*The
Reluctant Adventuress*

Fawcett Crest Books
by Sylvia Thorpe:

THE SWORD AND THE SHADOW
THE SCANDALOUS LADY ROBIN
BEGGAR ON HORSEBACK
THE GOLDEN PANTHER
ROGUES' COVENANT
SWORD OF VENGEANCE
CAPTAIN GALLANT
ROMANTIC LADY
THE RELUCTANT ADVENTURESS
FAIR SHINE THE DAY
TARRINGTON CHASE
THE SCARLET DOMINO
THE SCAPEGRACE
THE SILVER NIGHTINGALE

SYLVIA THORPE

The Reluctant Adventuress

A FAWCETT CREST BOOK

Fawcett Publications, Inc., Greenwich, Connecticut

THE RELUCTANT ADVENTURESS

THIS BOOK CONTAINS THE COMPLETE TEXT
OF THE ORIGINAL HARDCOVER EDITION.

A Fawcett Crest Book reprinted by arrangement
with Hurst and Blackett, Ltd.

Copyright © 1963 by J. S. Thimblethorpe.

All rights reserved, including the right to reproduce this book
or portions thereof in any form.

All the characters in this book are fictitious,
and any resemblance to actual persons living or dead
is purely coincidental.

Printed in the United States of America

The
Reluctant Adventuress

1

The post-chaise had left the main road some distance behind, and was following a narrow lane which wound its way deep into the Surrey countryside. Within the carriage a frosty silence prevailed. The two occupants sat gazing from their respective windows at the passing fields and hedgerows, the gentleman calmly, the lady with an air of curbed impatience, her elegantly gloved fingers drumming angrily against her knee. At length, as though able to contain herself no longer, she transferred her resentful gaze to her companion's face and expressed her feelings in no uncertain terms.

'God save us, how much farther must we travel on this wild-goose chase? I swear I would never have come with you had I known the half of it! Even if this scheme of yours is to be of the least help to us—which I take leave to doubt—you could surely have accomplished this part of it without my help.'

'My dear Cassy, you know very well that I could not,' he replied patiently. 'Miss Medway has always regarded me with suspicion, and would certainly not allow me to remove my niece from her charge unless I came accompanied by my wife.'

Cassy, an opulent and stylishly dressed blonde, also regarded him with suspicion. 'I thought you said the girl was no longer a pupil at this school, but a teacher?'

'To the best of my belief, she is. When I was last there Miss Medway had formed the intention of making Katharine her assistant when her education was completed, rather than send her as governess into some strange household. Remember, the child has been at Medway House since she was eight years old. Miss Medway will naturally still consider herself responsible for her.'

'I don't like it!' Cassy said bluntly. 'And, what's more, I don't understand it. Why did you never tell me of the chit till now? You say this grandfather of hers with the high-sounding name——'

'Sir Randolph Storne.'

'Aye, Sir Randolph Storne! You say he sent her to the school after her mother died, so that she might be educated to earn her own living when she was grown, but I've been about the world enough to know that titled gentlemen don't send their granddaughters as governesses unless there's something havey-cavey about 'em. Come, what's the truth of it? Is this girl a by-blow of your precious brother's?'

Duncan Murrell frowned at his wife in some annoyance. He was a distinguished-looking man with a handsome, world-weary face and a fine head of iron-grey hair, and was of an age to be the father rather than the husband of the good-looking young woman beside him.

'For God's sake, Cassy, set a curb on your tongue!' he replied irritably. 'You succeed in looking like a lady, so endeavour to act like one! As for Katharine, she is the lawful daughter of Charles Murrell and Priscilla Storne. It was a runaway match, though, and the old gentleman never forgave them for it. Priscilla was his only child.'

'An heiress, eh?' Cassy remarked cynically. 'Now I understand!'

'I doubt it!' Mr Murrell's tone was dry. 'Sir Randolph's estate was tied up in such a way that it could pass only to a male heir, and so he intended his daughter to marry the cousin who would one day inherit it. She was already betrothed to him when she met my brother, but within a month she and Charles were away to Gretna Green.'

'And the old gentleman, instead of coming up to scratch, turned them both out of doors,' Cassy concluded with a laugh. 'But how came a brother of yours to bungle such an affair? I'd have thought he would have made very certain first that the girl's fortune was secure.'

An ironic smile touched her husband's lips. 'Stranger still that such a consideration never entered his head. It was a love-match, my dear, which is something *you* will be unable to comprehend. To tell truth, I found it difficult to understand myself. Charles was twelve years my junior, and I had not reared him to set any store by romance.'

Cassy was frowning. 'If the old gentleman cast

his daughter off, how comes he to be paying for the girl's schooling?'

'Oh, that came much later, after both her parents were dead. He has never, to my knowledge, set eyes on Katharine. Had Priscilla borne a son it might have healed the breach, but the child was a girl, and Charles broke his neck in a curricle-race before she was six months old. I've a suspicion that the old man's bitterness was fostered by the kinsman Priscilla jilted. *He* never forgave her for making him look such a confounded fool, but he had his revenge in the end. She was obliged to go begging to her father for help, for Charles left her almost penniless and I could not afford to burden myself with an ailing woman and a child.'

'That I can believe!' Cassy interrupted. 'You have never burdened yourself with anything, have you, unless you could see some profit in it?'

He laughed. 'I am a practical man, Cassandra! I did the only thing I could for Priscilla, which was to approach Sir Randolph on her behalf. In the end he was prevailed upon to give her a small annuity on condition that he was never required to see her or the child. When Priscilla died he had Katharine sent to Medway House, and there she has remained ever since.'

'And, from what I know of you, she would be well advised to stay there,' Cassy remarked flippantly. 'How old did you say she is now?'

'Nineteen, or thereabouts, for I believe it is close upon three years since I saw her. Yes, I am sure of it! It was the summer of 'fifteen, and the whole country was celebrating the news of Waterloo. Katharine was sixteen then, and already showing promise of a quite remarkable beauty. Strange! Charles was well-looking in his way, but she does not greatly favour him, and Priscilla was nothing above the ordinary.'

Cassy paid very little heed to this irrelevancy, but continued to pursue her own train of thought. 'Suppose she does refuse to go with us?' she asked after a moment. 'A fine pair of fools we shall look if we have put ourselves to all the expense of this journey for nothing.'

'My dear Cassy, the girl is a Murrell! Of course she will go with us. If I am any judge of the matter she has been pining for years to escape from Miss Medway's establishment. You have not yet seen the place! Its precise gentility is truly overpowering.'

'That's another thing!' she retorted triumphantly. 'This girl has been bred to be a lady. What use are simpering airs and pretty accomplishments to us?'

'Of very great use, my dear, as you would see if you had sufficient imagination,' he replied amiably, 'but we will not quarrel over that. Your task is to make her welcome and win her confidence, and that should not be difficult. You are young enough for her to look upon you as a friend, and I am sure that she will be willing to be guided by your advice.'

'Maybe,' she said dubiously, 'but it is going to cost a pretty penny, you know. I dare say she has not one gown fit to be seen.'

He laughed. 'A trifle more expense, my love, cannot signify when we are already in so deep! It may even be the means of us making a recovery, for, as far as I can see, Katharine is the only asset left to us. Depend upon me to make full use of her.'

Mrs Murrell still seemed unconvinced, but when,

an hour or so later, she was confronted by Katharine in the prim parlour of Medway House, she was obliged to admit that in one respect at least her husband's judgment had not been at fault. The girl's beauty was breath-taking. A perfect, oval face with exquisitely modelled lips, and enormous, long-lashed eyes the colour of violets, was crowned by glossy black hair which escaped from its demure bands into rebellious curls. She was tall and gracefully made, with a full yet slender figure which not even an unfashionable, unbecoming gown of Miss Medway's providing could disguise, and bore herself with unselfconscious elegance. Cassy, blinking at this vision of loveliness, could at first think of nothing but the absurdity of its being wasted upon an exclusively feminine establishment.

They had already endured a somewhat trying interview with Miss Medway herself, a formidable lady whose frigid civility made no secret of the fact that their arrival was unwelcome. She had stared with obvious disapproval at Cassy's dashing attire and the remarkably bright gold curls clustering beneath the brim of her high-crowned, feathered bonnet, and shown a marked reluctance to summon Katharine into her presence. But Duncan Murrell had been courteously but firmly insistent, just as he had insisted upon talking to his niece in private, so that at last Miss Medway, rigid with offended dignity, swept out of the room and left the three of them alone.

Katharine, having greeted her uncle and made her curtsy to his wife, had been standing with downcast eyes and her hands clasped lightly before her, but she looked up uncertainly as the door closed.

THE RELUCTANT ADVENTURESS   13

Cassy smiled, and patted the sofa on which she was sitting.

'Now we can be comfortable! Come and sit down, my dear, and let us become acquainted,' she said invitingly, adding, as Katharine obeyed: 'My name is Cassandra and I make you free of it, but I'll not forgive you if you try to call me "Aunt".'

Considerably startled by this forthright remark, Katharine murmured an assurance that she would do nothing of the kind. To regard this stylish young woman as an aunt would, she thought, be utterly impossible. She had been astonished to hear of her uncle's marriage, and quite dumbfounded by her first glimpse of his wife. Good manners had carried her through the introduction, but she had experienced the utmost difficulty in tearing her fascinated gaze away from her new relative.

Her feeling towards her uncle was a curious one. She had seen him no more than a dozen times in her whole life, yet those few brief meetings had made a profound impression upon her, perhaps because he was the only man of her own class with whom she had ever been acquainted. Her mother she remembered only as a frail, complaining invalid, living frugally with only herself and an elderly maidservant for company. On rare occasions Duncan Murrell had visited their modest lodging, and with careless good humour made much of his little niece. When her mother died he appeared again, and bore Katharine off to a house in a different part of London, where she was spoiled and petted by a lady with a loud, good-natured laugh and very gay clothes. He had argued on her behalf with Sir Randolph Storne's lawyer, and when the old baronet's wishes were at last made known, escorted her to Medway House. Since that time, when his own affairs permitted and the thought occurred to him, he had come on two or three occasions to see how she did, but Miss Medway had not encouraged these visits. She held a poor opinion of men in general and of Duncan Murrell in particular.

'Well, my dear Katharine,' he said now, taking a seat facing the two ladies, 'you have done a deal of growing up since last I saw you. Miss Medway tells me that she finds in you a most able assistant.'

Katharine shook her head, a rueful smile quivering enchantingly about her lips. 'Indeed, sir, I would be happy to think so, but I fear that she said so merely to spare your feelings. She tells me to my head that I am idle and foolish and of an incurably frivolous disposition, and that she permits me to remain here only because it would be impossible for me to obtain an eligible post elsewhere.'

'Well, she's right in that, at all events,' Cassy declared roundly. 'No woman in her senses would take *you*, miss, into her house.' She saw the girl's suddenly stricken look, and added impatiently: 'God save us, child, have you no mirror? Looks such as yours would be no asset to a governess.'

The colour rose hotly in Katharine's cheeks. 'Indeed, ma'am, I cannot think———! Miss Medway has never suggested———' She broke off in confusion and looked beseechingly at her uncle.

'Miss Medway, I fancy,' he said kindly, 'has never encouraged you to think very much about your looks, but the fact remains, my child, that you are an exceedingly beautiful young woman. No, there is no need to blush! I speak no more than the simple truth.'

'Miss Medway says that beauty is a snare and a delusion,' Katharine remarked doubtfully, 'and that one should consider one's looks no more than is necessary to achieve a neat and proper appearance.'

'To be sure she does,' declared the forthright Cassy. 'If I had a face and a figure like hers *I* wouldn't want to consider them.'

This blunt remark betrayed Katharine into a giggle, but she stifled it immediately and looked guiltily about her. Mr Murrell frowned, not very severely, at his wife, and went on:

'I have no doubt that Miss Medway sought to instil such a belief into you, Katharine, because she considered it to be proper to the station in life which you have been educated to occupy. It is a lamentable fact that great beauty can be a grave handicap, and would be bound to prejudice any lady against employing you as a governess. But have you never thought, my dear, that you might prefer a different sort of life to the one you lead at present?'

Katharine sighed. She had thought it very often, as she listened to Miss Medway's pupils talking eagerly of their coming entry into society, and of the gaieties in store for them, but she had always known that her own destiny was very different. Miss Medway had never concealed from her the circumstances of her presence at the school, or that her grandfather's help would be withdrawn as soon as her education was completed.

'Sir,' she said in a low voice, lifting lovely, troubled eyes to his face, 'it would be idle to pretend that I have not dreamed of a life of a very different kind, but I know that for me it cannot be more than a dream. I have a living to earn, and I prefer to earn it here, where all is familiar, rather than to venture into a strange and possibly hostile establishment.'

'That is natural, my child,' he replied indulgently, 'and were there no other alternative I should commend your choice. But an alternative now exists. In the past I have been able to do very little for you. The circumstances were such . . .' A vague gesture completed the sentence, conveying at once everything and nothing. 'But now all that is changed. I have a wife, a house in London—in short, my dear child, there is a home awaiting you, and Cassandra and I have come to fetch you to it.'

'To—to fetch me? To London?' Katharine was stammering with astonishment and disbelief. 'Sir——! Uncle, you do not mean it?'

'Certainly I mean it, Katharine! You cannot suppose that, being at last in a position to provide for my brother's daughter, I should permit her to live anywhere but under my own roof? It is all arranged. We shall put up for the night at some convenient inn, to give you time to make your preparations for departure, and then drive back to town tomorrow.'

'Tomorrow?' Katharine repeated blankly. 'Sir, I do not know what to say! Your generosity and kindness—and yours also, ma'am—put me under an obligation which I can never hope to repay, but I do not see how I can leave Medway House so soon. It would put Miss Medway to a great deal of inconvenience, and she has been very good to me.'

'Perhaps, my child, but she has been amply recompensed,' he pointed out cynically, and Cassy added shrewdly:

'And I'll be bound she does not pay *you* overgenerously for teaching the brats.'

'I receive ten pounds a year, ma'am,' Katharine assured her earnestly, 'and Miss Medway provides me with clothes also.'

'Ten pounds?' Cassy repeated, outraged. 'God save us, one would think you were a servant-girl! And if that gown is an example she does not dip very deep into her purse to clothe you.'

Katharine flushed, and looked unhappily at her uncle. He said, with a decided edge to his voice: 'It seems to me, my dear Katharine, that Miss Medway has been guilty of imposing upon your inexperience. She may pretend that in persuading you to remain with her your welfare was her first concern, but I suspect *that* consideration to have rated far below her own interests. I think you need have no qualms at all about leaving her house with no more delay.'

'You may be right, sir,' Katharine agreed in a troubled voice, 'but she has been kind to me in her fashion, and I would not wish to part from her with any ill-will. Is it truly necessary for me to leave so very soon?'

A look of displeasure descended upon his face. 'My dear girl, we have put ourselves to the trouble of travelling from London for no other purpose than to invite you to make your home with us, and you cannot expect us to kick our heels in this out-of-the-way spot to suit Miss Medway's convenience. We both have many engagements in town, and since it would be ineligible for you to make the journey alone, I am afraid I must insist that you return with us tomorrow. Of course, if you choose instead to remain here there is no more to be said.'

'God save us, Duncan, there is no need to browbeat the poor child!' Cassy exclaimed with swiftly assumed indignation, putting her arm about Katharine's shoulders. 'Of course she will come with us, will you not, love? Never trouble your head on that old tabby's account! She will be well served for trying to turn you into a drudge.'

Katharine was not entirely convinced, but deliberately to turn her back upon the one chance of escape which had ever been offered to her required a greater degree of fortitude than she possessed. She begged her uncle's pardon, and gave him to understand that she would fall in with his plans.

It was not to be expected that Miss Medway, when the news was conveyed to her, would accept it with equanimity, but all her arguments and protests were swept aside by Mr Murrell. He did not hesitate to refer to the manner in which she had taken advantage of Katharine's inexperience, and the knowledge that she had indeed treated the girl unfairly robbed her protests of much of their authority. She parted from Mr and Mrs Murrell on distinctly unfriendly terms, and Katharine was enabled to face the evening with confidence only by the knowledge that it was the last she would spend at Medway House.

Duncan Murrell and Cassy bade her an affectionate farewell, assured her that they would return the following morning, and went off to bespeak rooms at the inn in the village. As the chaise emerged from the drive of Medway House into the lane, Mr Murrell turned to address his wife.

'Now that you have met Katharine, my dear, do you not agree that she is something quite out of the common way? The face of a madonna, the figure of a pagan goddess—and as innocent as though she had been reared in a convent! A remarkable combination!'

'It will be even more remarkable if she is still as innocent three months from now,' Cassy replied dryly. 'Oh, she's a beauty, right enough! Even dressed like a dowd, and with her hair scraped back so, she's the loveliest piece *I've* ever seen, but beauty's not the only consideration. What about the dreary hole yonder she's been mewed up in all these years? A rare training, that, for a life like ours!'

He shook his head. 'As I said before, my love, you are sadly lacking in imagination. Can you not see that her innocence, her air of breeding, allied as they are to such beauty, are the very qualities which will be of most use to us? We must move cautiously, of course! It will not do to shock or alarm her, but I have no doubt that, between us, we shall be able to achieve some arrangement highly satisfactory to all of us.'

'Except, maybe, the girl herself,' she retorted. 'Well, I am sure I hope you may be right, but don't be surprised if she takes fright at the first hint of the truth, and comes running back to that old harpy and her rubbishing school.'

Events were to prove, however, that this fear was groundless. Quite early on the following morning, while Mr and Mrs Murrell were still at breakfast in the neat parlour of the Stag Inn, a gig drove into the inn-yard, deposited on the doorstep Katharine, a battered portmanteau, and a small trunk which had seen better days, and then rattled off again. Mr and Mrs Murrell, having observed the incident from the parlour window, were regarding each other in mild perplexity when the door opened and Katharine herself came into the room.

A drab pelisse was buttoned up to her throat, for the spring morning was chilly, and her outmoded bonnet framed a pale and troubled face, but in spite of this she still looked remarkably beautiful. Her uncle, who had risen to greet her, said in a tone of some surprise:

'Why, Katharine, how is this? Did I not make it plain to Miss Medway that we intended to drive up to the school to fetch you?'

'You made it plain, sir, but Miss Medway was not disposed to allow me to await your arrival.' Katharine was tugging off her gloves as she spoke; both her voice and her hands were trembling. 'In short, I have been turned out of doors! She would have obliged me to leave last night, only it was too late to send to the farm for the gig.'

She broke off, unable to control her voice any longer, and Cassy got up and came to clasp the agitated hands in her own.

'God save us, child, your fingers are like ice! Come to the fire, do! Duncan, pour some coffee for her, for I declare she is chilled to the bone.'

She led Katharine to a chair by the fire and obliged her to sit down, while Mr Murrell filled a cup with coffee and brought it across to her. There was a gleam of satisfaction in his eyes, but Katharine was too agitated to perceive it, and his voice held nothing but indignation as he said:

'This, I collect, is to punish you for leaving her with so little warning. Upon my soul, I never supposed that she would sink to such petty vindictiveness!'

'I am afraid, sir, that I am a little to blame,' Katharine confessed. 'After your departure yesterday she kept plaguing me to change my mind, saying that I was giddy and ungrateful, and that I would regret flouting my grandfather's wishes in this fashion. She said such wicked things of you, and of Mrs Murrell, and of my poor papa—oh, I cannot tell you, but there was no bearing it! So in the end I told her that I cared nothing for Sir Randolph Storne, and had always resented being the object of such grudging charity as he has doled out to me, and that she had no right to speak so about my father's family. That made her angrier than ever, and she said that I might go to London, and good riddance, but I was not to come whining back to her if I found I was mistaken in you.'

'A charitable woman!' Mr Murrell commented dryly. 'How did you answer that?'

Katharine took a sip of coffee and set the cup down. A little colour had come back into her cheeks, and her eyes were sparkling with remembered anger. 'I told her, sir, that I would sooner starve than apply to her for assistance. That nothing on earth would persuade me to set foot again in a house where I and my relations were so poorly regarded.'

He laughed. 'Well said, my child! I am sorry

that you have been subjected to so distressing a scene, but it will not do to be dwelling upon it, you know. Endeavour to put it out of your mind, for you have done for ever with Miss Medway and her school. They have no place in the life which now lies before you. Am I not right, Cassy?'

'Oh, to be sure!' There was a sarcastic inflection in Cassy's voice, but Katharine did not hear it. 'That's the one thing about which there can be no doubt at all!'

2

The shadows were lengthening by the time they reached London, but to Katharine, who had not been more than ten miles from Medway House during the past eleven years, everything she saw was new and interesting. They crossed Westminster Bridge, seeing the river a sullen steel grey under the grey evening sky, and threaded their way northward through the busy streets until at last they came to a halt before one of the big houses in St James's Square. Mr Murrell, alighting, handed the ladies down, and his wife went briskly up the steps to the front door, Katharine following her in silent astonishment. She had supposed her uncle to live in a good part of the town, but she had not expected a residence as imposing as this. As they reached the door it was opened by a dignified butler, and Cassy led her guest into the hall, a stream of instructions and questions issuing from her lips the while.

'Has a guest-chamber been prepared, as I ordered yesterday? Oh, Foster, this is Mr Murrell's niece, Miss Katharine, who has come to stay with us. Is all in readiness for tonight? God save us, I thought we should be home before this—we shall scarce have time to swallow our dinner! Tell Maggie to lay out my lilac gauze, and the amethysts. She will have to dress me before she unpacks Miss Katharine's things.'

This monologue had carried them across the hall and up the first few steps of the handsome staircase. Katharine, following her hostess towards the first floor, said uneasily:

'I fear I have put you to a great deal of inconvenience, ma'am. Do I understand that you have an engagement tonight?'

'Yes, we are giving a card-party. That is why we could not delay any longer in Surrey, for it would not do for the guests to arrive and find neither their host nor hostess at home.'

They reached the top of the stairs, and through an open door Katharine caught a fleeting glimpse of a large, handsomely furnished saloon, with another, similar room beyond, but Cassy led her on without a pause, up another, shorter flight of stairs and into a comfortable parlour at the back of the house. Waving Katharine to a chair, she untied the long, satin strings of her bonnet, tossed the headgear on to the table, and shook out her blonde curls.

'God save us, look what time it is! I told your uncle we should have set forward earlier! We shall have the guests knocking upon the door before we have so much as changed our clothes.' She saw the look of dismay in Katharine's face and added reassuringly: "No need for you to come down to the saloons tonight, my dear. You can stay quietly up here and go early to bed, for I dare say you are tired from so much excitement, and you will not wish to go into company until you have something more becoming to wear. I would gladly lend you a gown, but I am a deal plumper than you, and besides, there is nothing in my wardrobe suitable for a young girl to wear.'

'Oh, indeed, ma'am, I would not impose upon you to that extent,' Katharine replied hastily, 'but it is quite true that I cannot go into company in any of the gowns I have. Your guests would think it exceedingly odd, I am sure, to see such a dowd in your house. I am very conscious of the appearance I present.'

Cassy laughed. 'As to that, child, I doubt whether any of the gentlemen would look twice at your gown, once they had clapped eyes on your face, but I understand very well how you feel. Never mind! Tomorrow I will take you shopping, and then you may be comfortable. But, for the Lord's sake, stop calling me "ma'am"! You make me feel at least fifty years old.'

Katharine, who had coloured faintly at Cassy's first remark, blushed more deeply than ever and hastily begged her pardon. 'I will try to remember, m——Cassy,' she added, 'but, you see, I have not been in the habit of calling anyone by their Christian name, except for the children, since the last of my friends left Medway House.'

Cassy, picking up her bonnet and casting another

harassed glance at the clock, had been moving towards the door, but at that she paused and turned to face Katharine again.

'You had a great many friends, I dare say', she remarked carelessly. 'Young ladies from families in the first rank of society?'

'I knew a number of the young ladies quite well, of course, but I had only one close friend among them, and that was Judith Tillingham.' She saw that this conveyed nothing to Cassy, and added in explanation: 'Lord Wedgeworth's only daughter, you know! She was my dearest friend, and when she first left Medway House she was used to write to me quite often, but Miss Medway put a stop to our correspondence. She said that it was foolish to pursue the acquaintance when our stations in life were so vastly different.'

'It seems to me,' Cassy said severely, 'that that old harpy was concerned only to cut you off from everyone, so that she might turn you into a drudge for her own profit.'

'Well, it did seem odd that she should be so set against my corresponding with Judith, for if I had tried to obtain a position as governess it would have been exceedingly helpful to have the recommendation of a lady of her rank.'

Cassy was swinging the bonnet by its ribbons, her gaze on the fluttering feathers. She said, still in the same careless tone: 'I suppose you do not know what has become of your friend?'

'Why, yes! She was married at the end of last year to Lord Elsdale. I saw the notice of the marriage in the newspaper, and wished very much that I could write to Judith to wish her happiness. Only Miss

THE RELUCTANT ADVENTURESS 27

Medway had forbidden me to correspond with her, and I could find no way of doing so without her knowledge.'

Cassy stared. 'Could you not even write a letter without her prying into it? God save us, your uncle was right when he said that you might as well have been reared in a convent! You will not find *me* so strict a chaperon, I promise you.' She broke off, seeming suddenly to recollect her previous haste. 'But come, child, and I will show you your room. We shall have plenty of time for chattering tomorrow.'

She led the way to a bedchamber more luxurious than any Katharine had ever seen, in which her trunk and portmanteau, which had just been carried upstairs, looked more dilapidated than ever. Nothing could have exceeded Cassy's kindness, but when Katharine insisted that she was quite willing to unpack without assistance she merely protested in a hurried and perfunctory way before hastening off. Katharine set briskly about the task of disposing her scanty possessions in wardrobe and chest of drawers, and since this was soon accomplished had time to dress her hair again, and change her travel-creased gown for a fresh one, equally plain and unbecoming, before Cassy's maid arrived to bid her to dinner.

Katharine stared, conscious of a good deal of surprise, for Maggie was not in the least like her mental picture of a fashionable lady's maid. She was an enormously fat old woman with a broad, red face and a voice as gruff as a man's, her vast bulk encased in a tight black gown. Studying Katharine with frank curiosity, she said bluntly:

'Well, Mistress said as you were a beauty, my dear, but she didn't tell me the half of it. There won't be one as can hold a candle to you once you're decently gowned. Bless my eyes if I ever saw skin so white or hair so black!'

Katharine, a little overcome by this fulsome praise of a beauty which she had been brought up to disregard, and startled to encounter such outspokenness in a servant, could find nothing to say. Maggie then bestowed upon her a beaming smile which revealed several missing teeth, and conducted her out of the bedchamber and down the stairs to the dining-room.

Here Mr and Mrs Murrell were awaiting her, he looking exceedingly distinguished in immaculate evening dress, she splendidly arrayed in gauze and silk. Katharine, who had an excellent eye for colour, could not feel that lilac and amethysts went particularly well with Cassy's bright golden hair and rather high complexion, and was secretly a little shocked by the amount of plump, smooth shoulder and bosom which the low cut of her bodice revealed, though she supposed that it must be the height of fashion. She remembered Cassy saying that she had no dress suitable for a young girl, and decided with relief that a more modest style would be more to her own taste.

When dinner was over, Mr and Mrs Murrell took their guest back to the parlour and settled her there with a pile of periodicals and a novel from the circulating library. Katharine, feeling sure that they must both be anxious to go down to receive their guests, was in the midst of assuring them that she lacked for nothing and would do very well, when the door opened and a young man walked without ceremony into the room.

He looked to be about twenty-eight years old, his tall, shapely person attired in a coat of somewhat dandified cut, a striking waistcoat, and long pantaloons strapped tightly beneath his insteps. Abundant, light-brown hair, slightly curling, was brushed into fashionable disorder above a handsome face with a beautifully shaped nose and somewhat sulky mouth, and he came into the room with all the assurance of one who was a frequent and welcome visitor.

'Bernard, my dear boy!' Mr Murrell greeted him jovially, shaking him by the hand. 'No one told us that you were here. We were just about to come down.'

'Oh, I have only just arrived. I came straight up.' The young man, who had been staring in a bemused fashion at Katharine, tore his gaze away with an obvious effort and moved forward to greet his hostess. 'How are you, Cassy? That's a devilish striking gown.'

'Oh, I am quite cast into the shade, and I know it,' she replied cheerfully, and turned to Katharine. 'My dear, let me make Mr Chard known to you. Bernard, this is Duncan's niece, who has come from Surrey to make her home with us.'

Mr Chard executed a graceful bow, and declared gallantly that Surrey's loss was undoubtedly London's gain. He spoke with a faintly mocking drawl, and though the frank admiration in his eyes brought the colour to Katharine's cheeks, she could not fail to notice that he was looking at her with a good deal of curiosity also. He showed a marked inclination to linger, but Mr Murrell said firmly that the guests would be arriving, and bore him off to the saloons below. Cassy stayed long enough to tell Katharine to ring for Maggie if there was anything she required, and then followed the two gentlemen downstairs.

Katharine sat turning over the pages of the periodicals and listening to the hum of voices which presently began to drift faintly to her ears from the saloons on the first floor. They seemed to be predominantly masculine, but she supposed that the softer tones of the ladies could not penetrate so far. The room was pleasantly warm, and the journey and the excitement of arriving in London had tired her more than she realized. After a while even the fashion-plates began to blur before her eyes, her eyelids drooped, and she sank into a doze.

She awoke with a start to find that the fire had burned low, and the hands of the clock on the mantelpiece stood at ten minutes to twelve. Startled to discover that she had slept for so long, and conscious of a chill due more to weariness than to the temperature of the room, she stooped to pick up the periodicals which had slipped to the floor, intending to place them tidily on the table before going to bed. As she straightened up with them in her hands, the door opened softly and Bernard Chard came into the room.

Katharine stared at him in surprise, and said, rather breathlessly: 'If you are seeking my uncle, sir, or Mrs Murrell, they are not here. I have not seen them since you all went downstairs.'

'I know!' He came farther into the room and closed the door behind him. 'They are still in the saloons, but you must be bored to death sitting here by yourself. I've come to keep you company.'

Astonishment deepened into a faint uneasiness, but she said with as much composure as she could muster: 'That is obliging of you, Mr Chard, but it is very late and I was just about to retire.'

'Late?' He cast a careless glance at the clock, and laughed. 'My dear girl, it is not yet midnight! The evening's entertainment has scarcely begun.'

Katharine was prepared to believe that an hour which was considered shockingly late at Medway House might be looked on very differently in London, but she could not feel that it was proper to be alone and unchaperoned with a gentleman at any hour. The suspicion crossed her mind that Mr Chard was drunk, but if that were the case he carried his wine remarkably well.

'Nevertheless, sir, I am on the point of retiring,' she said firmly. 'I am not accustomed to travelling, and it has made me very tired. I must beg you to excuse me.'

She put the periodicals down on the table and went towards the door, expecting him to open it for her, but he did not move. He was studying her with a faint frown, and once more she could see perplexity in his eyes. He said, with the air of one making an unexpected discovery:

'Good God! Don't tell me you really are Duncan's niece!'

This seemed such a ridiculous thing to say that for a moment she could only stare at him in bewilderment, almost certain now that he was in his cups. 'But of course I am,' she said at length, in the reasoning tone she would have used to one of her erstwhile pupils. 'My father, Charles Murrell, was his younger brother.'

'I never knew Duncan had a brother.'

'He died when I was a baby,' she explained patiently, 'and my mother when I was eight years old. That is why my uncle and his wife invited me to live with them. Now, if you will have the goodness to let me pass . . .'

He paid no heed to this, but merely said, with a faint lift of the brows which seemed to indicate that he found her explanation incredible: 'If you were orphaned as a child, where has he kept you hidden all these years?'

Katharine began to feel both angry and alarmed. He was still standing squarely in front of the door, and much as she would have liked to escape from the room, she was reluctant to make any attempt to push her way past him.

'I cannot perceive, Mr Chard, that it is any concern of yours,' she said as calmly as she could, 'but until yesterday I was at school in Surrey.'

'At school?' His glance flickered appraisingly over her before returning to her face. There was a sceptical look in the dark eyes. 'Deuce take it, my dear, you are no schoolgirl!'

'Oh, this is intolerable!' she exclaimed, her feelings getting the better of her at last. 'If you do not stand aside this instant I shall ring for the servants. And if you wish to inquire any further into my circumstances, Mr Chard, I suggest that you address your impertinent questions to my uncle.'

He appeared to be considerably taken aback by this, and stared at her very hard for a second or two. Then he recovered his countenance and said with a sneer:

'Perhaps I will, for it's plain *you* are not disposed to answer them. It's a dashed queer turn-out, as far as I can see, and I'll lay odds you don't know the half of it. I'll bid you good night then, since you are so curst unfriendly, but I warn you that we're likely to see a good deal of each other if you stay here.'

He lounged out of the room without waiting for a reply, and Katharine, considerably puzzled and not a little alarmed, retreated hurriedly to her bed-chamber. Tired though she was, it was some time before she was able to sleep. She could not put Mr Chard's curious behaviour out of her mind, and derived no satisfaction at all from the prospect of closer acquaintance with him.

By morning, however, these misgivings seemed absurd, and she was even able to put the disquieting incident out of her mind for a time. Bernard Chard must have had too much to drink, and as long as his behaviour gave her no further cause for complaint she would say nothing of what had occurred. It would scarcely be a good start to life in her uncle's house to be on bad terms with someone who was obviously his close friend.

As soon as breakfast was over Cassy kept her promise to take Katharine shopping, and the whole morning was spent in this delectable pursuit. They returned home with the carriage piled high with packages, to find Bernard Chard with Mr Murrell. Katharine gave him a rather wary look, but he greeted her civilly and said that he had come to ask them all to be his guests that night at the masquerade to be held at Covent Garden. He had hired a box there, and invited his friend Tom Catterbury and his sister to join the party.

To Katharine, the mere word 'masquerade' conjured up a picture of gaiety and excitement, but Mr Murrell seemed at first to be oddly reluctant to allow his niece so rare a treat. After a while, however, under the spur of Cassy's and Bernard's persuasion, and Katharine's disappointed face, he relented, merely stipulating that it should be left to him to decide at what point they should leave the assembly.

Cassy had arranged for a hairdresser to come that afternoon to cut Katharine's hair into a fashionable style, so that by the evening, when Maggie had helped her to dress, she found a stranger looking back at her from the mirror. An astonishingly beautiful stranger, with raven curls twisted into a high knot on the crown of her head and framing her face with artless ringlets. A stately creature in a gown of hyacinth-blue gauze over a satin slip, with a spangled scarf draped across her arms, and pearls belonging to Cassy glimmering at her throat.

Bernard came to dine with them, and the look in his eyes when she came into the room told Katharine that the mirror had not lied. All through dinner she was aware of his regard, and was almost thankful when the time came for her and Cassy to withdraw, leaving the gentlemen to their wine.

Before setting out for Covent Garden they all put on the masks which Cassy produced, and this, to Katharine, lent an immediate air of mystery and romance to the evening which arrival at their destination did nothing to dispel. The great Opera House, its interior glittering with crimson and white and gold, with painted ceiling and crystal chandeliers, would have been impressive enough under any circumstances to one reared in a country village, but now, filled as it was with a brilliant, shifting crowd clad in every colour of the rainbow, it was a sight to take the breath away. Many of the revellers were in fancy dress, others in dominoes of every hue, while others, like Mr Chard's party, contented themselves with ordinary evening dress and merely hid their identities behind masks. Some had dispensed even with this formality, and though most of these were gentlemen, Katharine saw several unmasked ladies, and marvelled that they should care to make themselves so conspicuous.

Bernard had hired a box in the second tier, and his two other guests were already waiting there for the rest of the party to arrive. Mr Catterbury was a willowy young man with a receding chin, his sister a petite brunette in pink, and both stared so hard at Katharine when she was introduced to them that she felt thankful for the protection of her mask.

This initial shyness soon wore off, and by the time supper was served she had danced several times with Bernard and with Tom Catterbury, and acquitted herself well enough to win praise from both gentlemen. A trifle intoxicated by this, and by the excitement of her very first ball, she paid little attention during supper to what was going on beyond the confines of the box, and when the meal was over hesitated only a moment when Bernard begged her to partner him in a waltz. It was only when they reached the stage, where the dancing was in progress, that she began to take notice of the standard of conduct of their fellow merry-makers, and to be shocked by the startling lack of decorum which was becoming evident. She started to say that after all she would rather return to the box, but Bernard paid no heed and, setting an arm about her waist, swept her into the dance.

The waltz was still considered daring by some old-fashioned folk, but since Miss Medway prided herself on neglecting no aspect of her pupils' education, Katharine had long since mastered all the steps, though practising in the schoolroom with one of the other young ladies as partner was very different from dancing with a gentleman on the crowded stage of the Opera House. She was not at all sure that she liked being held in the manner demanded by the dance, but very soon realized that Bernard was holding her a good deal more tightly than was strictly necessary. When she tried to draw back he merely drew her closer to him. All her earlier mistrust returned, and though a single glance about her showed that he was by no means alone in his reprehensible conduct, this did nothing to lessen her shocked alarm. She struggled to free herself, but he only laughed and made no attempt to slacken his hold.

'Don't be foolish, my dear,' he said softly, his lips close to her ear. 'Cassy told me you'd had a devilish strict upbringing, but you're not in your curst schoolroom now.'

'I wish to Heaven I were,' she retorted. 'Mr Chard, I insist upon being taken back to the box immediately, and if you do not let me go this instant I shall complain to my uncle of your conduct.'

A little to her surprise, but to her profound relief, his clasp on her waist slackened. He said sulkily:

THE RELUCTANT ADVENTURESS 37

'Oh, very well, but where's the harm? Let me tell you that you will be obliged to forget these strait-laced notions if you are to live in Duncan Murrell's house.'

'That is evident, sir,' she retaliated swiftly, 'if all his friends share *your* peculiar standards of behaviour.'

'So you've a temper, have you?' He looked down at her, his eyes slightly narrowed. 'Take a word of advice, my dear, and learn to hide it.'

'I do not need your advice, Mr Chard, nor do I desire it. What I *do* desire is to be restored immediately to my uncle's protection.'

For a moment he continued to study her flushed and angry face. Then he laughed. 'You've a deal to learn yet,' he said lightly. 'Very well, I'll take you back, but I'll wager that in a few months' time you'll be less high in the instep.'

They were now free of the circling dancers, and with a gesture of exaggerated courtesy he offered his arm, and led her up the stairs and along the corridor to the box. Katharine, her head high and her cheeks still burning hotly below the mask, maintained a dignified silence to cloak a growing disquiet, for there seemed to be some meaning behind her companion's words which she did not understand. She would not look at him, but sensed that he was watching her with mockery in his eyes.

When they reached the box they found that the party had been increased by the arrival of one lady and three gentlemen, who had encountered Mr Catterbury and his sister as they went to join the dancers, and so diverted them from their purpose that they had all returned together to the box. More wine had been called for, and there was a great deal of talk and laughter. The newcomers hailed Mr Chard with shouts of welcome, the lady, a plump redhead with a green domino over a very daring gown, going so far as to clasp both hands about his arm and declare in tones of mock reproach that he had not been near her for an age.

They all stared at Katharine, who made haste to slip into a chair at her uncle's side. He cast her a searching glance but made no comment, apart from urging her to take another glass of wine, which she did not want but was reluctant to draw further attention upon herself by refusing. Her head ached, and all that she now desired was to leave a party which was fast becoming as unruly as the rest of the assembly, but an attempt to catch Cassy's eye met with no success. Mrs Murrell was sitting a little withdrawn from the rest, closely engaged in conversation with the gentleman who was leaning over the back of her chair.

He was the only member of the party not wearing a mask, and the face thus revealed was dark-complexioned and bold of feature. He looked to be about thirty-five, tall and heavily built, and could have been considered handsome in a rather coarse and obvious way. As Katharine watched him he turned his head and favoured her with a long, appraising look, then bent and said something in Cassy's ear. She replied, and he then made some further remark which made her laugh, and rap him across the knuckles with her folded fan.

Mr Murrell followed the direction of his niece's glance, and for a moment his gaze rested thoughtfully upon Cassy and her companion, until a shriek of laughter from the redheaded girl drew his attention towards her. Bernard had sat down and pulled her on to his knee, and now bestowed on her a kiss to which she readily responded. Katharine, hot with embarrassment, sat with downcast eyes, and then with profound relief heard her uncle say quietly:

'This party, I think, has ceased to be amusing. Would you care to return home, Katharine?'

She turned thankfully to him. 'Oh yes, if you please! But will the others not think it excessively odd?'

'What they may think is not of the smallest importance,' he replied quietly. 'Where is your cloak?'

This being found and placed around Katharine's shoulders, Mr Murrell then led her across to his wife. The dark man straightened to his full height as they approached, but Cassy made no attempt to rise from her chair, and merely eyed them with resentment.

'God save us, Duncan!' she said pettishly. 'You do not mean to leave so soon?'

'Katharine is tired, my dear, and has the headache. You must remember that she is new to town life. Moreover, I warned you this morning that I should leave as soon as I considered it advisable.'

Cassy tossed her head and turned a petulant shoulder. 'Leave then!' she snapped. 'I shall do very well without you.'

Katharine gasped and shot a startled glance at her uncle, but he continued to regard his wife with unimpaired calm.

'I do not doubt that, my love! I shall take the carriage, for I am sure I may depend upon Bernard or' —with a faintly satirical glance at the dark man—'or Ormsby to bring you safely home. Come, Katharine!'

Bernard had the grace to rise to his feet as they bade him a brief good night, but he still kept one arm about the redhead's shoulders, looking at Katharine with a mocking expression in his eyes. As the door of the box closed behind them, Katharine heard the other girl give a shriek of laughter which she felt certain was at her expense, and her cheeks burned again.

They did not speak, except to exchange the merest commonplaces, until they were in the carriage and clattering through the dark streets. Then Katharine, who had been turning over in her mind the events of the evening, said in a diffident voice:

'Uncle, is Mr Chard related to Cassy?'

'Related to her?' he repeated. 'No! Why do you ask?'

'Well, he seems to be upon such terms of intimacy with you both, and I had never heard of any relations of that name on our side of the family. I thought perhaps he was a cousin, or some such thing.'

Mr Murrell did not reply at once, and she wondered uneasily whether she had offended him. 'I have known Bernard Chard for a number of years,' he said at length, 'and he is very often in my house. Cassy, too, has a kindness for him. But if he has said or done anything to distress you, Katharine, I beg that you will tell me.'

'Oh no!' she exclaimed. 'How could I? It is not for me, sir, to censure your friends.'

'True,' he agreed, 'but you are in my charge now, and it is my duty to protect you. You are a very beautiful girl, and Bernard no less susceptible than any other young man. Possibly he thinks that the terms on which he stands with me, the fact that I have long treated him as a member of my family, give him the right to behave towards you with a greater degree of familiarity than is generally allowable.'

He paused inquiringly, and Katharine hesitated, torn between a desire for reassurance and reluctance to be the cause of any disagreement between the two men.

'His manner does seem to me a little free,' she said carefully at length, 'but no doubt I am refining too much upon what has occurred. I know so little of the world, and what may seem shocking to me is perhaps nothing of the kind, and should not be regarded.'

'Perhaps,' he conceded dryly, 'but it is far more likely that Bernard's conduct is at fault. I shall speak to him on that head, but do not fear, my child, that we shall quarrel over it. He and I know each other far too well for that, and it will only be necessary for me to make the situation plain to him. Rest assured that I shall do so without delay.'

3

It had seemed to Katharine that there must inevitably be some awkwardness attached to her next encounter with Cassy, but if Mrs Murrell felt this to be the case she gave no sign of it. When the two ladies met over a belated breakfast she made no mention of the masquerade, but began to talk instead of further shopping which must be done. As soon as they rose from the table she ordered the carriage and once more bore Katharine off to the shops where she selected lengths of muslin and cambric, laces and ribbons and branches of artificial flowers, saying that Maggie should make up dresses for her.

'And you need not fear, love, that she will make you look a fright,' she added reassuringly. 'I do not mind telling you that she has been making clothes for me for years. Well, we have bought enough for the time being, I think, so we had best be getting home. I mean to take you walking in the Park this afternoon, for every person of fashion walks or rides or drives there. On a fine day like this, you may see the whole world, I dare say.'

Katharine correctly interpreted this large statement to mean the whole of the Polite World, and a few hours later was able to see for herself that it was no exaggeration. The Park was very pleasant on that mild spring day, with primroses and crocuses in full flower, the daffodils just breaking into bloom, and a mist of new green on the trees. The carriageway was thronged with riders, and with vehicles of every type from the staid landaulet to the sporting curricle, while groups of elegantly dressed people strolled along the paths, or paused to chat with chance-met acquaintances.

Katharine was enchanted by the whole animated scene, and, secure in the knowledge that she was looking her best in a cherry-red pelisse over a dress of white muslin, and a cherry velvet bonnet with a high brim which most becomingly framed her face, was able to hold her head as high as any lady in the Park. She attracted a good many curious and admiring glances, but was too interested in all that was going on around her to pay much heed to them. Cassy, looking unwontedly demure today in a muted shade of green, pointed out all the notables to her, but it seemed at first as though none of her own acquaintances were taking the air that day. Then, as they strolled along a winding path between flowerbeds, they came face to face with a slightly built, elderly gentleman who, after one swift glance at Katharine, immediately swept off his hat and bowed.

'My dear Mrs Murrell, this is a delightful surprise! I was informed—erroneously, as I now perceive—that you had gone out of town.'

'We *have* been out of town, my lord, but only long enough to fetch Mr Murrell's niece from Surrey,' Cassy responded, and turned to her companion. 'Katharine, my dear, allow me to make Lord Carforth known to you.'

'Your servant, ma'am!' His lordship bowed again, and then put up his quizzing-glass and through it studied Katharine intently. 'Enchanting!' he murmured. 'Quite enchanting! Mrs Murrell, you are to be congratulated.'

Katharine, acknowledging the introduction, thought that this was a curious thing to say. She was not sure that she liked being so closely inspected, but decided that it would be foolish to take offence, since Lord Carforth was probably old enough to be her grandfather. He was dressed with a quiet and unobtrusive elegance which, in its very lack of ostentation, hinted at great wealth, and his thin, lined face with high-bridged nose and arrogant mouth wore the look of a man who had never needed or endeavoured to please anyone but himself. Nothing could have exceeded the courtesy of his manner, but encountering the glance of those cold, cynical grey eyes, she was conscious of an inward shrinking for which she could find no rational explanation.

He walked with them for several minutes, talking pleasantly and entertainingly, and parted from them only when they reached the promenade bordering the carriageway. Katharine was glad to see him go, and was about to make some inquiry concerning him of Cassy when she was astonished to hear her own name spoken in an excited feminine voice.

'Kathy! Katharine Murrell! I had no notion you were in town!'

Katharine turned quickly. The speaker was a pretty, fair-haired girl, very stylishly dressed, seated in an elegant open barouche which was drawn up at the edge of the carriageway. A young man who stood beside the carriage, and with whom the fair girl had evidently been talking when she caught sight of Katharine, had turned to look in the same direction, and now bore all the appearance of one who had been stunned.

Katharine gasped, and an expression of such delight swept over her face that the young man blinked as though dazzled. She ran forward until she stood beside him, looking up at the girl in the barouche.

'Judith!' she exclaimed rapturously. 'Oh, I hoped so much that I might see you again, but I never dreamed that it would be so soon.'

Judith leaned down from the carriage to clasp the proffered hand. 'Nor I,' she declared. 'But how is this, Kathy? I fancied you still at Medway House, and could scarcely believe my eyes when I saw you walking by.'

'Oh, I have come to London to live with my uncle and his wife. You remember my uncle, Judith? He came sometimes to Medway House to see me.' She broke off as Mrs Murrell, who had followed her at a more decorous pace, came up to them. 'Cassy, this is my friend Judith Tillingham— Lady Elsdale, that is—of whom I was telling you the other day. Judith, my—my aunt, Mrs Murrell.'

A look of surprise passed fleetingly across her ladyship's face, and then she smiled and held out her hand. 'I am happy to make your acquaintance, ma'am. Katharine will have told you what close friends we were when we were at school. But we cannot talk comfortably here. May I not take you up with me for a turn about the Park?'

'I am agreeable,' Cassy replied promptly, 'for, to be sure, your ladyship and Katharine must have a deal to talk about. She knows no one in town yet, for she has been here scarcely two days, and she is a trifle lonely, are you not, love?'

Judith smiled. 'I well remember my own first days in London! I thought I would never grow accustomed to it.' She became aware of the gentleman who still lingered expectantly close by, and gave a little laugh. 'Oh, Edward, I beg your pardon! This surprise has so scattered my wits that I had forgot you were there. Mrs Murrell, Katharine, pray allow me to introduce my brother, Mr Tillingham.'

The Honourable Edward Tillingham bowed, and declared with profound sincerity that he was delighted to make their acquaintance. He then handed them up into the barouche, and directed towards his sister a look of mingled entreaty and command. She disregarded it, saying kindly but with finality:

'I shall look to see you then, Edward, at the theatre. Pray convey my compliments to Lady Ainwood, and tell Fanny that I hope to see her during the interval.'

In the face of this heartless dismissal he could only bow again, and step back as the barouche moved off. Waving him an airy farewell, his sister said with a chuckle:

'Poor Edward! He wished me to invite him to go with us, for I could see that he was much taken with you, Kathy! But we could not talk comfortably if he were by.'

Katharine laughed, but blushed a little also. 'How absurd you are, Judith! Why, I scarcely exchanged half a dozen words with your brother.'

'Good gracious, my dear, with your looks you do not need to!' her ladyship retorted irrepressibly. 'But do not let us waste time talking of Edward. It is delightful that you are come to live in London—I have wished so many times that you were here. I would have invited you to visit me, you know, but I knew that odious Miss Medway would never permit it.' She turned impulsively to Cassy. 'Do you know, ma'am, she would not even allow Katharine to correspond with me? I may tell you, Kathy, that I had quite made up my mind to drive down one day to call upon you. I have spoken to Elsdale about it, and he had not the least objection.'

She rattled on in this style for several minutes, and soon drew Katharine into animated conversation. Cassy said very little, allowing the two girls to chatter to their hearts' content, but she covertly studied Katharine the while. This reunion with her old friend had quite banished her air of shyness. She was talking and laughing, her eyes sparkling and her cheeks delicately flushed, and looking so beautiful that it said much for Lady Elsdale's generosity of disposition that a great part of her conversation was concerned with plans for the entertainment of her friend.

'But the wretched thing is, Kathy, that we can do none of these things immediately, for I am going out of town tomorrow,' she confessed at length. 'You must know, my dear, that Elsdale's grandmama, who is very old, and lives in Denbighshire, of all impossibly remote places, has expressed a desire to make my acquaintance. Well, to be frank with you, she has been badgering us to visit her ever since we were married, but Elsdale has fobbed her off with the excuse that it is far too long a journey to make in the middle of winter. Now, of course, we can delay no longer. I own that I am shaking in my shoes at the prospect of meeting her, for I am told that she is a very strict old lady who disapproves most strongly of any kind of frivolity, so I do not suppose for one moment that she will approve of *me*. And to make matters worse, there are any number of other relations living in that part of the country whom we shall be obliged to visit also, and we cannot hope to be back in town for weeks.'

Some of Katharine's animation deserted her at this, for the prospect of having Judith's company in the immediate future had made her feel a great deal happier. Glancing at Cassy, she thought that she, too, looked a good deal put out, and was further discouraged by the possibility that Mrs Murrell had been hoping for Lady Elsdale to relieve her of some of the responsibility of entertaining her. Innocent though she was, Katharine had already guessed that Cassy was a woman upon whom the society of her own sex would soon pall.

Judith, observing her friend's downcast expression, and casting about in her mind for some means of alleviating the disappointment, hit upon a happy idea. Turning to Cassy, she said eagerly:

'Mrs Murrell, I know it is shockingly short notice, but if you have no *very* pressing engagements this evening, will you permit Katharine to dine with us,

THE RELUCTANT ADVENTURESS 49

and go with us to the theatre? It will be only a very small party. Just myself and Elsdale, and a gentleman who served in the same regiment with him in Spain and Flanders, and who has only recently returned to this country. We plan to see the play, and to have supper afterwards at the Piazza. Do say that Kathy may come! I promise that I will take very good care of her.'

'Oh, Cassy, please!' Katharine turned to her with parted lips and shining eyes. 'I should like it above all things, and you have not made any plans for this evening, have you?'

'Nothing from which you cannot be excused, my dear,' Cassy responded readily. 'Your uncle is entertaining some friends at home, but he will have no objection, I am sure, to your accepting Lady Elsdale's invitation. To be sure, it would be unkind to deny you, when you have not seen your friend for so long.'

So it was arranged, and her ladyship then very civilly offered to convey her companions home. There they parted, Judith to return home to Berkeley Square, and Katharine to hasten indoors to prepare for the evening's entertainment.

She went straight to her room, while Cassy, having ascertained that Mr Murrell was at home, went to inform him of Lady Elsdale's very flattering invitation. When she rejoined the younger woman, with the information that Mr Murrell had no objection to the projected plan, she found her standing in some indecision before her open wardrobe.

'Cassy, which dress should I wear? The blue gauze?'

'God save us, child, you are not going to a ball! Wear the rose pink, and the velvet cloak.'

Maggie, summoned to assist Miss Murrell, performed her task with her usual extraordinary deftness, and it was a very stylish and beautiful young lady who was presently driven in her aunt's carriage to Berkeley Square. Since Judith was expecting only two guests, she dispensed with all formality and came to meet Katharine in the hall, going with her to lay off her cloak. She was looking very charming herself in pale blue silk, but made no secret of the fact that she felt herself to be completely overshadowed by her friend.

'I declare, Kathy, I had forgotten how lovely you are,' she said with affectionate frankness. 'You will be the rage of London within a week, and that odious Arabella Marcham, whom all the gentlemen are foolish enough to call "the Peerless," and who gives herself such airs as a result, will be quite cast into the shade. Alas, that I shall not be here to see it!'

'Judith, what a goose you are! You have not changed in the least,' Katharine protested, laughing. 'I own I look prettier than I did at Medway House, but that is because of the way I am dressed. No one could fail to look well in such clothes as my uncle has bought for me.'

'If you believe that, it is very plain that you are new to town,' her ladyship replied bluntly. 'Why, I could show you a dozen girls, all dressed as becomingly as you, who are such shocking frights—but there, I must not be uncharitable! Let us go and join the gentlemen before my tongue completely betrays me.'

THE RELUCTANT ADVENTURESS 51

Katharine laughed again, remembering that Judith's unruly tongue had led her into countless scrapes during her schooldays, and the laughter was still lingering in her face as she followed her hostess into the drawing-room. The two gentlemen who were sitting there rose to their feet as the ladies entered, and looked at Katharine with admiration, but she was unaware of it, or of Lord Elsdale, a pleasant-faced man in his early thirties, coming forward to greet her. She was staring past him at the younger, taller man in the background. Staring incredulously, with a panic-stricken sense of unreality, for Lord Elsdale's military friend was Bernard Chard.

4

She scarcely heard his lordship's words of greeting, or knew what she murmured in response, so great was her bewilderment, so many and so wild the possible explanations which darted through her mind. It was Bernard, and yet in some mysterious way it was not, and there was no glimmer of recognition in his eyes. As in a dream she saw Lord Elsdale beckon him forward, heard him beg leave to present Captain Chard.

'*Captain* Chard?' she repeated dazedly. 'I do not understand.'

'Kathy!' Judith's voice was eloquent of concern. 'What is wrong?'

'If I might hazard a guess, Lady Elsdale,' Captain Chard put in calmly, 'I would say that Miss Murrell has already met my brother.' He turned to Katharine with a smile. 'Pray do not look so alarmed, ma'am. You are not the victim of a delusion. I am Brandon Chard. Bernard is my twin.'

'Oh!' Katharine said faintly. 'Oh, I see!' The explanation was surprising, but prosaic compared with some of the suspicions which had flashed into her mind, and she felt uncomfortable as she thought of them. 'Forgive me, sir, but the likeness is truly astonishing, and I am so little acquainted with Mr Chard that I was not aware he had a brother, much less a twin.'

A trace of irony crept into the Captain's smile. 'It is not a point which he would consider worthy of mention, Miss Murrell. In fact, he and I have not even met for a number of years.'

Katharine did not know what to reply to this, and instead regarded the Captain in silence. Now that the first shock of seeing him had passed, she realized that although the likeness between the brothers was strong enough to seem almost uncanny, there were also subtle differences. The slightly curling brown hair, the dark eyes, the beautifully modelled nose—these were identical, but where Bernard's mouth was sullen, lending a look of discontent to the whole countenance, Captain Chard's expressed both strength of will and humour. He was a little taller and broader than his brother, with a soldierly air about him, and affected a less dandified style of dress. Finally, a small scar slanting above his right eyebrow distinguished him unmistakably from his twin.

Brandon Chard, meanwhile, was regarding Katharine as intently as she was studying him, his dark eyes warm with admiration. She became aware of it, and of the fact that she had been staring at him in a very ill-bred manner, and the colour rose in her cheeks.

'I beg your pardon, sir,' she said hurriedly. 'You must think me excessively impertinent to stare you out of countenance in this fashion. I am sorry.'

His lips twitched, and the eyebrow with the scar rose a fraction, quizzically. 'My dear ma'am,' he replied gravely, 'I, too, was guilty of staring, but I am quite sure that *my* pleasure far exceeded yours.'

Katharine blushed more deeply than ever, but Judith gave a little gurgle of laughter.

'Very neat,' she said appreciatively, 'but pay no heed to him, Kathy. I have been acquainted with him for only a very few days, but I have already discovered that he is a shocking tease.'

'Lady Elsdale, you wrong me!' he protested. 'You cannot deny that I have just spoken no more than the simple truth.'

Still laughing, she shook her head. 'You know very well what I meant, sir, and I retract not one word of it. Am I not right, Elsdale?'

'Quite right, my dear, but you will do very much better not to cross swords with Chard. He is by far too expert a fencer for you to engage with.'

'Flattery, Robert!' Brandon retorted with a smile. 'No degree of skill could avail against so charming an adversary.'

Fortunately, since Katharine was quite unaccustomed to this sort of light-hearted banter, and felt incapable of bearing any part in it, the butler chose at that moment to announce dinner. Lord Elsdale offered her his arm, while Captain Chard took Judith in, and it was with some relief that she presently found herself at table. A good deal of her earlier shyness had returned, but Judith, in spite of her new status as a matron and a peeress, was still so much the merry companion of her schooldays, and Lord Elsdale so kind in a quiet and reassuring way, that it was impossible to remain for long ill at ease. As for Captain Chard, although Katharine still found his likeness to Bernard a little unnerving, she could not fail soon to realize that the resemblance was no more than superficial. In Bernard's presence she could not feel comfortable. There seemed always to be some hidden meaning in his words, and a hint of malice, as though he were perpetually at odds with life and eager to wound or offend those about him. In Brandon's manner there was no indication of so ugly a trait. He was amiable and amusing, and it was plain from their conversation that he and Elsdale were close friends and that his lordship held him in very high regard.

From the talk at the dinner-table she gathered that he, too, would be leaving London next day in order to visit his home, and that, since this was situated in Worcestershire, he intended to travel with the Elsdales as far as that county. This knowledge caused her to feel a faint pang of disappointment and dismay; it seemed that she was fated to be deprived of new acquaintances as well as of old friends.

When they reached the theatre it soon became evident that Judith at least had no reason to fear loneliness, for her friends and acquaintances seemed innumerable. They had barely entered their box before she was smiling and bowing to people in other parts of the house, and drawing her husband's attention to the presence of this person or that. Captain Chard placed a chair for Katharine, relieved her of her cloak, and then, sitting down beside her, remarked with a wry smile:

'It seems to me, Miss Murrell, that we strangers to London had best support each other. I trust you do not find it too lowering to the spirits to be unable to detect acquaintances in every other box?'

'I will confess, sir, that it would be delightful to claim so large a circle of friends,' she replied in the same light tone, 'but *you*, I am persuaded, are not upon your first visit to London.'

'The first for seven years, ma'am, and that is an absence long enough to make anyone feel a stranger. When last I was here it was as a very junior officer on furlough from the Peninsula, at which time, no doubt, many of these elegant young ladies and dashing gentlemen were still in the schoolroom. That is a reflection calculated to make one feel one's age.'

She laughed, but regarded him with some curiosity. 'Lady Elsdale said that you and Lord Elsdale were in the same regiment, sir,' she remarked. 'I collect that your military duties have kept you out of England all this while?'

He shook his head. 'No, Miss Murrell, I have no liking for peace-time soldiering. Elsdale and I sold out at much the same time, soon after Waterloo, but for vastly different reasons. He had just succeeded to the title, and came home to assume the responsibilities attendant upon it.'

'And you, Captain Chard?' she prompted shyly as he paused, and he laughed.

'Oh, I have no responsibilities at all, ma'am, and no desire for any. Elsdale will tell you that I am a feckless fellow, wholly lacking in sterling qualities.'

'I am sure he would tell me no such thing,' she protested with a smile. 'I do not know, of course, but surely, Captain Chard, to be an army officer is to accept a very grave responsibility?'

He shrugged. 'Perhaps,' he said lightly, 'but that is a very different matter, you will agree, from the kind of responsibilities of which we were speaking. They would not do for me at all. To tell truth, Miss Murrell, I am a great deal happier knowing that I am free to roam about the world than I would be in Elsdale's position, in spite of its many advantages.'

'Yet you have come home, sir, after all.'

'For a time, Miss Murrell, until I weary of it again,' he replied with a laugh. 'I was in Italy, but I had a sudden fancy to see another English spring.' His dark eyes were intent upon her face. She was aware of it, even though her own gaze was directed towards the curtained stage. 'Now I am glad that I came, for one forgets how much beauty is to be found here. Almost enough, I swear, to tempt a man to remain.'

It was at this interesting point in the conversation that Judith chose to intervene, and Katharine did not know whether to be glad or sorry. Her ladyship, directing her friend's attention to a box directly opposite their own, and at the same time smiling and waving to the party at that moment arriving in it, remarked:

'There is Edward, with the Ainwoods! Sir Joseph is a neighbour of Papa's, Kathy, and we have been friends all our lives. I must make you known to Lady Ainwood, and to Fanny, who is a most amiable girl. That is she, on the left.'

Katharine, looking towards the box, saw that an imposing dowager had now taken her seat there, and was directing the disposition of the rest of her party. Miss Fanny, a slight and rather colourless young lady in a very demure gown, returned Judith's smile, and Mr Tillingham, encountering Katharine's glance, bowed very deeply. Lady Ainwood inclined her head graciously to the Elsdales, looked very hard at their companions, and then beckoned Edward Tillingham to her side.

'Inquiring who you are, no doubt,' said the irrepressible Judith. 'She has three unmarried daughters besides Fanny, you know.'

Fortunately the curtain was raised at that moment, and Katharine forgot everything else in rapt enjoyment of the first play she had ever seen. To her it was entirely wonderful, and though Lord Elsdale might describe it as a very indifferent piece, and Judith allow her attention to wander to other parts of the house, she remained completely absorbed throughout the first act. Captain Chard seemed equally attentive, and if his glance turned more often to Katharine's face than to the stage, she was this time totally unaware of it.

When the curtain fell at the end of the act it became immediately apparent that numerous gentlemen had suddenly discovered in themselves an urge to pay their respects to Lady Elsdale. At least half a dozen of them invaded the box during the first few minutes of the interval, so that Lord Elsdale, indulgently surveying the crowd, caught Captain Chard's eye and led the way to the corridor at the rear of the box.

'I begin to think it fortunate that we *are* going out of town in the morning,' he said pensively as they sauntered along. 'Judith is apparently determined to try her hand at match-making, and the prospect of the tactics which she may see fit to employ is truly unnerving. I would like to think that by the time we return her friend will be creditably established, but I fear there is not the least likelihood of it.'

The Captain shot him a curious glance. 'Disapprove of Miss Murrell, Robert?' he inquired.

'Not in the least,' his lordship replied calmly. 'She appears to be as amiable as she is beautiful, but neither quality is likely to prove sufficient to establish her creditably, for I understand that she has no fortune whatsoever. Judith tells me that she was educated for the purpose of becoming a governess.'

Brandon regarded him suspiciously. 'Are you bamming me, Robert?' he demanded severely.

'Certainly not! I own the notion seems absurd when one looks at her, but Judith assures me that such is the case. However, it may be that this uncle of hers will do something for her. I know nothing of him, but it would appear that he is comfortably circumstanced.' He paused, and then added abruptly: 'No need to speak of this to anyone, Brandon. Wouldn't add to the girl's consequence.'

'Since when, my dear Robert, have you had cause to suspect me of being a gabster?' his friend asked resignedly. He was silent until they reached the end of the corridor and turned to retrace their steps. Then he said thoughtfully: 'I'm not sure that I agree it is a good thing you are going out of town. I have the oddest feeling that Miss Murrell would be glad of your wife's support.'

'Good God!' Elsdale stopped short and put up his glass, studying the Captain with the liveliest astonishment. 'Never tell me that you, of all people, are thinking of casting your handkerchief in that direction?'

'Don't be a fool, Robert!' Brandon replied amiably. 'You know damned well that *I* am not hanging out for a wife, even if she were rich as well as beautiful. *That* is an encumbrance which I have no intention of acquiring.'

'No,' said his lordship dryly, 'but I sometimes think it would be a dashed good thing if you did.' He dropped the glass to the length of its ribbon, but then lifted it again immediately to regard the young gentleman who was approaching from the opposite direction. 'Ah, Edward! Have you, too, come to make the acquaintance of the new beauty?'

'If you mean Miss Murrell, I met her in the Park this afternoon,' Mr Tillingham replied. He nodded to the Captain. ' 'Evening, Chard! No, I came to tell you that Lady Ainwood desires you all to come to her box for a few minutes.'

'Impossible, my dear boy!' With a wave of the quizzing-glass Elsdale indicated the door of his own box, which stood open to reveal the throng within. 'Half the bucks in the theatre were before you. Pray tell her ladyship that we will avail ourselves of her invitation after the second act.' Mr Tillingham hesitated, obviously reluctant to accept his dismissal, and his brother-in-law added kindly: 'I will convey the message to Judith.'

Thus deprived of any excuse to linger, Edward cast him a darkling glance and took himself off, while Elsdale, chuckling, re-entered the box to fulfil his self-imposed errand. Brandon followed and, skilfully circumventing two attendant gentlemen, regained his place at Katharine's side. She looked up at him with so warm a smile of welcome in her lovely eyes that he was conscious of a momentary stirring of something more than admiration, while the two gentlemen instantly and severally decided that they detested him.

As soon as the second act was over Judith rose to her feet, saying that they must go to Lady Ainwood's box immediately, before anyone else came to theirs, and giving her companions no time to make any protest. Her ladyship welcomed Judith affectionately and Elsdale and Captain Chard with complaisance, but though Katharine was greeted graciously she was subjected also to a long and critical scrutiny. Lady Ainwood, who had had an excellent view of the gentlemen thronging the Elsdale box during the first interval, now discovered that Judith's friend was even lovelier at close quarters than when seen from a distance, and the knowledge did nothing to commend Miss Murrell to her. No mother of four hopeful daughters could welcome the arrival of so dazzling a beauty upon the social scene.

Lady Ainwood being one of those domineering mothers who allowed her daughters neither opinions nor personality of their own, Fanny merely acknowledged the introductions, and even Judith's affectionate greeting, with diffidence before sinking back into her chair. She made no voluntary contribution to the conversation, speaking only when directly addressed, but her gaze rested upon Katharine with a kind of despairing envy, and wistfully upon Edward, who had attached himself to Miss Murrell as soon as she entered the box. Captain Chard, a perceptive man, observed both the envy and the wistfulness, and moving to her side did his best to engage her in conversation, but though she responded politely it was plain to him that her attention was still elsewhere. Her mother cast her one or two exasperated glances, but no one else appeared to notice her lack of spirits.

Lady Elsdale's party remained with the Ainwoods almost until the end of the interval, but did not encounter them again that evening, which was rounded off very agreeably by a delightful supper-party. Katharine thought that she had never enjoyed herself so much in her life. Lord Elsdale was a kind and thoughtful host, Judith her usual merry, madcap self, and Captain Chard—Katharine was not quite certain what she thought of Captain Chard. It was impossible not to compare him with his brother —greatly to Bernard's disadvantage—and he was undoubtedly both handsome and charming, but she could not help feeling a little shocked by his devil-may-care attitude towards life.

It was an attitude which Katharine had been brought up to look upon as deplorable. Her earliest memories were of her mother's fretful voice complaining endlessly of the irresponsibility of the husband who had left her destitute, and these complaints had impressed themselves deeply upon Katharine's childish mind. Nor had her long sojourn at Medway House done anything to erase them, since Miss Medway's views were very similar to those of Charles Murrell's widow, and she had not hesitated to point out to his daughter on numerous occasions the dire consequences of such unstable ways. Katharine imagined that her father must have been just such a man as Brandon Chard.

No, she could not entirely approve of him, but neither could she deny that she found him very likable, or wholly stifle a feeling of disappointment that he was leaving London so soon. The Captain, it seemed, found in this fact equal cause for regret, and when the carriage drew up outside Mr Murrell's house, although it was Elsdale's place as host to conduct Katharine to the door, did not hesitate to forestall him. Both gentlemen alighted while the ladies were taking an affectionate leave of one another, but his lordship had barely handed Katharine down before Brandon offered her his arm. Elsdale's brows lifted a little, but he merely said with a smile:

'I see that I am quite cut out, and that, if I may say so, in a most underhanded fashion. Good night then, Miss Murrell. We have found great pleasure in your company, and look forward to enjoying it again when we return to town.'

She smiled shyly back at him, thanked him for a delightful party, and allowed the Captain to lead her up the steps to the door. His lordship re-entered the carriage, and informed his wife that there was no need for her to look like a cat at the cream-jug. Brandon Chard was an accomplished flirt, and if she was hoping to make a match between him and Miss Murrell she was doomed to disappointment.

The accomplished flirt, meanwhile, waiting for the door of the house to be opened, was telling his fair companion how much he deplored the ill luck which was taking him out of London the moment he had made her acquaintance, and begging leave to call upon her as soon as he returned. Katharine, blushing rosily and looking adorably confused, assured him that he would be welcome, and added innocently:

'For you will wish, of course, to communicate with your brother. I am afraid that I have not his direction, but my uncle, I am sure, will be able to supply it.'

He looked down at her, a twinkle in his dark eyes, the quizzical eyebrow lifted. 'No doubt I *shall* be obliged to encounter Bernard sooner or later, but I assure you, Miss Murrell, that I do not find the prospect anywhere near as alluring as that of seeing *you* again.'

The door was opened by Foster, and the light from within flooded over them. Brandon took Katharine's hand and kissed it, and then with a murmur of farewell she went past the butler into the house. Captain Chard, ignoring the incredulous stare which Foster had fixed upon him from the moment of opening the door, and which he had no doubt was due to his likeness to Bernard, returned to the waiting carriage.

Katharine paused in the hall, looking about her in some surprise. From Cassy's words she had formed the impression that only a few guests were expected, and yet the house bore all the appearance of being the scene of a large party. Candles burned everywhere, in chandeliers and in wall-sconces; from a room on her left came a murmur of voices and a subdued clatter of dishes and cutlery; a

THE RELUCTANT ADVENTURESS 65

waiter emerged from the back of the house and went up the stairs, carrying bottles of wine and glasses on a tray.

Faintly puzzled, Katharine, too, began to go slowly upstairs, loosening her cloak as she went. She was not quite certain what to do, not wishing to thrust herself upon her uncle's guests and yet equally reluctant to seem lacking in civility. At the top of the stairs she paused, but the voices which could be heard in the large saloon seemed to be exclusively masculine, and she decided to go in search of Cassy before venturing in. As she turned to go, the waiter came out of the saloon again and hurried away, leaving one leaf of the door open and so revealing to Katharine a scene so unexpected that she forgot her original intention and instead went slowly forward until she stood in the doorway.

The saloon was a large and handsome room, its tall windows closely curtained with crimson brocade, two huge, glittering chandeliers depending from the lofty ceiling, and its furniture consisting largely of tables, and chairs with curious wooden stands beside them, the purpose of which appeared to be to hold wine-glasses and what looked like rouleaux of coins. At several of these tables gentlemen sat at cards, while at one end of the room a group about a larger table was apparently also intent upon some game. At the other, Cassy, in a gown of pale yellow satin, presided over another table where a wheel shaped like a rimmed bowl was spinning, and absorbing the whole attention of the persons gathered about it.

Katharine stood and stared, a frown wrinkling her brow, her astonished gaze passing from one group to another while her own presence went unobserved. So intent was she upon the scene before her that she failed to hear the approaching footsteps, and turned with a start and a little cry as a hand grasped her arm above the elbow and Bernard Chard's voice said softly, in a tone of malicious amusement:

'So now you know what I meant last night when I said that you'd be obliged to forget your strait-laced notions! You didn't know the half of it, did you, when Duncan and Cassy invited you here? I'll lay odds you would never have come if you had known then that your uncle keeps a gaming-house!'

5

Although the words merely confirmed what she had already guessed, this did nothing to lessen Katharine's shocked dismay. As her stricken gaze returned to the saloon, the mocking voice beside her went on:

'You'll observe that he is presiding over the faro-table, and Cassy at the roulette wheel. I told you you had a deal to learn yet! Now, what else can I tell you about our establishment? Picquet, hazard, deep basset—we provide for them all, as you will also have to learn. Oh yes, and we keep a betting-book, in case any of our guests wish to record a wager.'

Katharine continued to stare wide-eyed at the scene before her. Her instinctive desire was to escape, but Bernard's grip on her arm was firm enough to prevent this, and before she could make any attempt to free herself one of the men standing by the roulette table happened to glance in her direction. For a second or two he stared, and then left the group and came strolling across to the door, and Katharine saw that he was the big, dark man who had joined their party at the Opera House the previous night.

'So Murrell's charming niece condescends to join us after all,' he remarked, 'and since neither he nor Chard troubled themselves to present me last night I must needs do so myself. Jack Ormsby, ma'am, entirely at your service.'

He bowed as he spoke, and Katharine was obliged to sketch a curtsy in response. She had no desire for a closer acquaintance either with Mr Ormsby or her uncle's gaming-rooms, but supposed vaguely that it would not do to snub one of the patrons.

'I am happy to meet you, sir,' she murmured, 'but I must beg you to excuse me. I was but passing the door—I had no intention of intruding.'

'Intruding?' he repeated with a laugh. 'I may tell you, my dear, that my only purpose in coming here tonight was for the pleasure of seeing you without that confounded mask. And what did I discover? That you had deserted us in favour of some other entertainment! Now I must insist that you join us, and there's not a man in the room who will not thank me for it.'

He offered his arm as he spoke, and Katharine, not knowing what to do, cast a despairing glance at Bernard, only to realize at once that he had no intention of rescuing her from this predicament. He had let go of her arm, but now stood behind her in the doorway so that to thrust past him would result

THE RELUCTANT ADVENTURESS 69

in an undignified scuffle which must surely draw unwelcome attention upon them. Bestowing upon him a look of angry reproach, she placed her hand reluctantly on Mr Ormsby's arm and allowed him to lead her forward into the room. Bernard, grinning, strolled after them.

Mr Murrell and Cassy caught sight of her at much the same moment, but even if they had felt inclined to come to her support, neither was free to do so. Mr Ormsby led her to a sofa at the far end of the room and seemed prepared to give her his undivided attention, but it was not long before all the gentlemen who were not actually engaged in play showed a marked inclination to drift in the same direction. Bernard stationed himself at Katharine's side and seemed bent upon making her known to as many of them as possible, but she was far too upset and agitated to feel any gratification at the compliments which were showered upon her.

A fleeting glimpse of her uncle showed that he was frowning in evident annoyance, but Cassy was hidden from her view by the men now clustered around the sofa. After a few minutes, however, Katharine heard her call in a very peremptory tone to Bernard to come and take her place, and as soon as this was done she bore down upon the group around Katharine. Skilfully ousting Mr Ormsby from his place, she sat down beside the girl and said brightly:

'I did not know, love, that you were come in! Did you enjoy your party?'

'Yes! Yes, thank you, it was delightful!' Katharine's tone was despondent, for the present situation spoiled the evening even in retrospect. She did not like the way in which some of the men were looking at her, and though Cassy's lips were smiling, her eyes were hard and bright with anger. 'But —but I did not mean to walk in upon *your* party, Cassy. I am sorry.'

'No need to apologize, my dear,' Jack Ormsby put in before Cassy could reply. 'Not for something which gives us all so much pleasure.'

'God save us, Jack, you will turn the child's head altogether!' Cassy declared rather shrilly. 'Pay no heed to him, Katharine, or to any of them. They will flatter you shamelessly, and mean not one word of it.'

There was a chorus of protest at this, and a good deal of jesting and laughter. Mr Murrell's frown deepened, and with a murmur of apology to those still at the faro-table he got up and came across to join the group around the two women.

'So you spent an agreeable evening, my child?' he said to Katharine, but did not pause for an answer. 'Well, that is excellent, but it will not do for you to tire yourself unduly, for you are not yet used to our London ways. I think it would perhaps be well if you were to bid the company good night.'

There were more protests, but Katharine was too thankful for the excuse thus offered to escape from the saloon to pay any heed to them. Saying gratefully that she was indeed very tired, she got up from the sofa and laid her hand on his proffered arm, pausing only to say a brief good night to Cassy and the gentlemen before allowing him to lead her towards the door. Bernard glanced up from the roulette wheel as she passed and bade her a cheerful good night, but she made no reply and only cast him a very speaking glance.

She was not to make her escape without one more interruption, for as she and her uncle drew level with one of the smaller tables a gentleman rose from his seat there and barred the way. It was Lord Carforth.

'Surely you are not leaving us again so soon, Miss Murrell?' he said pleasantly. 'I was hoping to improve upon the acquaintance which we began in the Park this afternoon. Murrell, can you not prevail upon her to stay?'

The words were a request, the tone a command. Mr Murrell hesitated, and for a moment Katharine feared that he meant to obey it. She cast a beseeching glance at his lordship, and found the cold eyes in that thin, lined face contemplating her with an expression which woke in her a sudden, indefinable dread. Her fingers tightened involuntarily on her uncle's arm, and as though this brought him to a decision he said, politely but with some firmness:

'I would be happy to oblige you, my lord, in any other matter, but my niece is feeling the effect of a long and tiring day. Nor has she, I am sure, the smallest interest in gaming.'

'That will not do, my dear fellow, in a niece of yours,' Carforth replied with a sneer. 'We must endeavour, must we not, to arouse that interest?' He turned again to Katharine. 'I will not detain you now, ma'am, but I shall look forward with uncommon eagerness to becoming better acquainted with you.'

She was obliged to murmur some polite reply,

but could not rid herself of an uncomfortable and probably unreasonable conviction that there was a threat implicit in the words. He stepped aside to let her pass and Duncan led her to the door, but when they reached the wide landing outside the saloon and she turned quickly towards him, he checked whatever she was about to say by a quick shake of the head.

'No, my child, this is neither the time nor the place. You shall talk to me tomorrow.'

He patted her hand and then lifted it from his arm and turned away. The doors of the saloon closed once more behind him, and Katharine stood for a moment staring at them, and listening to the murmur of voices and laughter from beyond. Then she turned and went slowly and unhappily to her bedchamber.

She did not ring for Maggie to come to her, but locked the door, dropped the velvet cloak on to a chair, and sat down before the dressing-table, staring at her reflection in the mirror. A gaming-house! Never in her wildest imaginings had she pictured herself in such surroundings, for only the most innocent of card-games had ever come her way. She knew, of course, that gambling was very common among fashionable people, but it was a severe shock to discover that her uncle, far from being a gentleman of independent means as she had supposed, made his living by catering for a human weakness which she had always been taught to deplore.

Many of the things which Bernard Chard had said to her, and which had seemed inexplicable at the time, were now unpleasantly plain. His attitude, and that of the other men in the gaming-room, made it quite clear that no one expected to find a respectable female in such a house as Duncan Murrell's. Innocent Katharine might be, but she was not a fool, and she had no difficulty in perceiving the difference between their bearing towards her and that of the gentlemen whom she had met while in Judith's company.

Sudden tears flooded her eyes as she thought again of the evening which had been so enjoyable at first and which had ended in disaster. There could never be another like it, for it was inconceivable that Lord Elsdale would permit his wife to continue upon terms of intimacy with a girl who lived in a common gaming-house. Nor was there any hope that he would not discover the truth, for all the patrons of Duncan Murrell's rooms had the appearance of men of fashion, and Lord Carforth was by no means the only gentleman of title among them. In the small world of fashionable society someone would be bound to recognize her, or Brandon Chard would come seeking news of his brother, and Bernard's malicious nature delight in betraying her true circumstances to him, and thus to the Elsdales.

By morning Katharine had decided that the only honest course was to write to Judith, telling her the truth and explaining that it would not be possible for them to meet again. Then, at least, no one would be able to accuse her of imposing upon her ladyship, or of using their childhood friendship as the means of insinuating herself into genteel company where she had no right to be. She was very much afraid that this was what her uncle and Cassy had intended, and therefore determined to despatch the letter surreptitiously as soon as an opportunity occurred.

Maggie brought a breakfast-tray to her room, and Katharine was thankful for the excuse thus offered to delay the inevitable meeting with Mr and Mrs Murrell. It was certain, she felt, to be distressing. When at last she went reluctantly down to the parlour she found it empty, but just as she was beginning to hope that they had both gone out, Maggie appeared again and asked her to step into Mrs Murrell's dressing-room.

She went unwillingly, and found there not only Cassy but Mr Murrell also, apparently absorbed in the perusal of a newspaper. He put this aside when she came in and rose to greet her, and she could detect no change at all in the urbane kindliness of his manner. Cassy regarded her critically.

'I thought a good rest would put new heart into you,' she observed, 'but it seems I was wrong. You look positively hagged.'

'Is that so remarkable, ma'am?' Katharine demanded, stung by this lack of perception. 'Do you imagine that I slept well after what I learned last night?' She swung round to face her uncle. 'Oh, why did you deceive me?'

He made a slight, rueful gesture. 'Would you have come to London, my child, if I had told you that I keep a gaming-house?'

'You know I would not! Oh, I do not mean to censure you, sir! I have no right to do that, but you must know that *I* can have no place in such an establishment.'

'And what's wrong, miss, with a gaming-house?'

Cassy demanded in a hard voice. 'You are obliged to earn a living, and if you think it better to do so by spending your days caring for a parcel of brats and being treated little better than a servant you must be hen-witted!'

'Hush, Cassy!' Mr Murrell said quietly, and came to take Katharine by the hand and lead her to the sofa. Sitting down beside her, he continued reasonably: 'My dear child, do but consider for a moment! What did the future hold for you except an inferior position in Miss Medway's school or some genteel household? To be, as Cassy says, little better than a servant? It is true that I cannot offer you a place in the first rank of society, but here you will at least be upon the fringe of the fashionable world. You will wear pretty clothes, go to balls and theatres, meet any number of interesting people. Can you truthfully deny that such a life is preferable to the dreary one your grandfather intended for you? *He* could have given you everything—wealth, position, a brilliant marriage—and he has refused to even acknowledge your existence. I, on the other hand, offer you all that lies within my power to give.'

Katharine hesitated, glancing from him to his wife. Mrs Murrell had picked up a hand-mirror and was peering closely at her reflection, having apparently lost interest in the conversation, but Katharine suspected that she was more attentive than she pretended. There was a subtle difference this morning in Cassy's attitude towards her, a hint of animosity which Katharine was at a loss to understand.

'Do not think, sir, that I am not grateful,' she said after a little, her troubled gaze returning to her uncle's face. 'I am sure that your intentions were excellent, but I do not know how to go on in an establishment of this kind, and you would find me a sad burden. It will be better if I do not stay.'

He shook his head. 'I believe, my child, that you have no choice. Did you not tell me that you parted from Miss Medway upon such terms that you can never return to her house? You can expect no help from your grandfather, and Cassy tells me that even your friend, Lady Elsdale, has gone out of town for a time.'

Katharine stared at him, her cheeks paling as she realized the truth of what he said, the ultimatum behind those kindly spoken words. The picture he had sketched of life in his house was not unattractive, but she felt instinctively that there was much which he had left unsaid. She was certain, too, that he had some purpose in bringing her to London other than concern for her, though she could not yet guess what it might be. Yet whatever it was she had no choice but to fall in with his wishes, and try to make the best of circumstances which filled her with misgiving.

'I could not apply to Judith for help, even if she were still in London,' she replied at length in a low voice. 'It was not well done of you, sir, to allow me to accept Lord Elsdale's hospitality while keeping me in ignorance of the truth.'

'Perhaps not,' he admitted, 'but do me the justice of remembering that the invitation was not of my seeking.'

'Uncle!' Katharine spoke calmly, the twisting together of her hands the only betrayal of inward agitation. 'Will you tell me one thing? If Lord Elsdale had been aware that you keep a gaming-house, would he have permitted Judith to invite me into his home, or to go with them to the theatre?'

There was a pause. Cassy laid down the mirror and turned slightly in her chair so that she could look at the two on the sofa. Duncan Murrell opened his snuff-box and inhaled a pinch with the utmost deliberation.

'No,' he said quietly at length, 'he would not. I will not try to deceive you on that score, Katharine. Elsdale might come to this house, and be upon the friendliest terms with you, but he would not permit his wife to receive you. I am sorry, my dear, but that is the kind of absurd prejudice against which it is impossible to fight. I am sorry, too, for the manner in which you discovered the fact of my profession. It was not my intention to thrust you without warning into the gaming-rooms, and Bernard knew it. You may be sure that I have taken him severely to task on that account.'

Katharine drew a deep breath. 'Mr Chard's position in this house is a little difficult to understand,' she said levelly. 'Perhaps you will be good enough to explain it to me.' She raised her eyes and looked steadily at her uncle. 'If I am to remain here, sir, I think I have a right to know.'

'You have every right,' he agreed promptly, 'but it is a position which is a trifle difficult to define. Bernard has lodgings in Ryder Street, but spends much of his time in this house. He assists us in the running of the establishment, for he, too, finds it necessary to augment a very small income. He is, in fact, as I told you the other night, almost one of the family. I fancy you do not greatly like him, but I must ask you to regard him with as great a degree of complaisance as you find possible. If you do not let him see that his conduct vexes you you will, I think, learn to deal tolerably well together.'

'Bernard is a born mischief-maker, and that's the truth,' Cassy added indulgently. 'There's some quirk in his nature that prompts him to it.'

Katharine turned a direct gaze upon her. 'So I had already remarked, ma'am,' she said quietly. She hesitated for a moment, and then said to her uncle: 'Are you aware, sir, that he has a twin brother?'

'Aye, we know it,' Cassy said sharply before her husband could reply. 'But what do you, miss, know of Bernard Chard's brother?'

'I met him last night. He is a friend of Lord Elsdale, and served in the same regiment before selling out.'

They stared at her in the utmost astonishment, and Mr Murrell said: 'I thought Brandon Chard was still abroad. He has not been in England for years. I wonder what brings him back now.'

'Whatever it is, it will be a sad blow for Bernard!' Cassy added with a titter. 'He has scarcely recovered from the disappointment of his brother surviving the war, and has been hoping ever since that some accident would befall him.'

'You cannot be serious!' Katharine exclaimed in a shocked tone. 'His own brother?'

'God save us, child, there's no love lost there!' Cassy replied cynically. 'You see, although they are twins, Brandon was the first-born and inherited their father's estate. Bernard has never forgiven him for it, though from all accounts it was no great prize. Just an old house and a few hundred acres of land! But Bernard could not bear a more bitter grudge if it were a dukedom.'

'Perhaps,' Katharine suggested timidly, 'he is very deeply attached to his home and resents his brother's long absence from it.'

Mr Murrell laughed. 'You give him too much credit, my dear! Bernard's only concern for the place is that it represents a few more thousands to be squandered as he has squandered every penny that has ever come into his hands. He has not been near it these ten years, and if he inherited it tomorrow would gamble it away within a twelvemonth.'

'What is this Brandon like?' Cassy asked curiously. 'We have never seen him.'

'In looks, he is astonishingly like his brother!' Katharine spoke briefly, already regretting that she had mentioned Brandon Chard at all. 'I could detect no other resemblance. Captain Chard is most gentleman-like.'

Cassy tittered again, and even Mr Murrell looked amused. 'And does he propose to call upon you, my dear? I should like to be prepared, for if Bernard encounters him we are likely to have a brawl on our hands.'

'He did say something of the kind,' Katharine admitted reluctantly, 'but I understand that he also is going out of town today.'

'In that event we need not put ourselves about on his account,' Mr. Murrell replied, getting up from the sofa. 'For the rest, do not distress yourself too deeply, my dear Katharine, over what may seem to you to be a deplorable state of affairs. You will soon accustom yourself to our ways, and since you are now committed to this life, endeavour to learn to enjoy it. Believe me, for Charles Murrell's daughter that should not be difficult.'

6

This cynical but eminently practical piece of advice did not promise to be easy to follow, but Katharine, realizing the futility of regret, determined to do her best. Cassy spent the rest of the morning describing to her the manner in which the house was run, and telling her a little about the more popular games. Later, she said, Katharine must learn to bear a part in some of these, but for the present it would be sufficient for her to appear in the saloons or keep the guests company at supper.

'For with your looks it will not matter if you do not know one card from another,' she said with a touch of scorn. 'You saw how they all flocked round you last night. They will come here on your account and, once here, will easily be persuaded to gamble, but remember! I want no missish airs or tears or vapours if a man shows that he admires you.' She saw that Katharine was beginning to look a little scared, and added impatiently: 'God save us, I do not mean that anyone will go beyond what is proper, but you cannot expect to be treated here as though you were still in the schoolroom!'

'I do not expect it, ma'am,' Katharine retorted sharply, 'and it was made abundantly clear to me last night that neither can I expect to be treated with even an ordinary degree of propriety. You must forgive me if I find the manners obtaining in this house a trifle too free for my taste.'

'In your high ropes, aren't you?' Cassy said sarcastically, but she did not sound altogether displeased. 'Oh well, a trifle of spirit never comes amiss, for the most beautiful woman can seem insipid without it. You'll grow accustomed to our ways after a few nights in the gaming-rooms.'

'Is there gaming here every night?' Katharine asked with some dismay.

'More often than not,' Cassy replied. 'We call them private parties, of course, and send out cards of invitation, but we welcome anyone with money to spend. You need not be thinking, though, that if you receive a flattering invitation to some other kind of entertainment we shall expect you to refuse it on that account. The more you go about, and the more people you meet, the better pleased we shall be.'

Katharine made no reply to this. She was beginning dimly to perceive the purpose behind her own introduction to the house, and knew that if she had been plain, or even no more than passably pretty, she would have been left at Medway House and soon forgotten. But Duncan Murrell had been quick to see that a beautiful niece would be a potent lure to draw gentlemen into his gaming-rooms, and deliberately whisked her away from Miss Medway's care with an abruptness which was bound to cause that formidable lady the deepest offence.

During the afternoon Cassy insisted that they should once again walk in the Park. Katharine went reluctantly, hoping that she would not encounter any of the people to whom Judith had introduced her, for she could not rid herself of a guilty feeling that she had met them under false pretences. Even the intimidating Lady Ainwood, however, would have been preferable to the company in which she presently found herself, for they had not been five minutes in the Park before they were joined by Jack Ormsby.

It was a meeting which made several things plain to Katharine. Mr Ormsby expressed surprise as well as pleasure at seeing them, but any doubt she might have had that the encounter was less fortuitous than it seemed was dispelled by Cassy's demeanour. All her vague ill-humour instantly vanished; she became suddenly very animated, talking and laughing with more vivacity than Katharine had yet seen her display. From the moment Ormsby joined them she ignored the younger woman completely, except when he tried to include her in the conversation. Then she bestowed upon her a look of such venomous resentment that Katharine was quite startled, and realized that Cassy looked upon the flashily handsome Mr Ormsby as her exclusive property. It was not a conquest which Katharine felt disposed to envy.

They were strolling beside the carriageway when, to her dismay, she saw Edward Tillingham driving towards them in a very smart perch-phaeton drawn by a pair of beautifully matched horses. Since he caught sight of her at the same moment she was obliged to bow, but any hope she might have had that this would content him was soon shattered. He drew up beside them, and after greeting Cassy and being made known to Mr Ormsby, begged leave to take Miss Murrell up beside him for a turn about the Park.

Katharine would have liked to decline the invitation, not only because she felt it would be wrong to encourage Edward's attentions, but because the sporting carriage, with its body suspended so high above the ground, looked to her inexperienced eyes a singularly perilous vehicle. But since Cassy was emphatically assuring Mr Tillingham that she would be delighted to entrust her niece to his care, and the groom had already jumped to the ground, she had no choice but to agree. With some misgivings she allowed herself to be helped up into the phaeton, and after engaging to return her to Mrs Murrell in a quarter of an hour, and telling his groom to wait for him, Edward gave his horses the office to start. Mr Ormsby watched the phaeton bowl away and then turned to walk on beside Cassy, casting her a sapient glance.

'That's Wedgeworth's eldest son, isn't it?' he remarked. 'You and Murrell are aiming high, my dear!'

Katharine, meanwhile, had been unable to restrain herself from clutching at the side of the carriage, for the ground seemed to be flashing past at dizzy speed a long way below. Edward glanced at her and grinned.

'No need to be frightened, Miss Murrell,' he said reassuringly. 'I won't overturn us, I swear!'

'No, I am sure you will not,' she agreed hastily, 'but you must know, sir, that I have never before had an opportunity of riding in such a carriage as this.'

'You will soon grow accustomed to it,' he assured her confidently, 'for I hope to have the pleasure of taking you driving very frequently. I must tell you, ma'am, that it's a dashed good thing I chanced to meet you today, for I had forgotten that Judith was going out of town and never thought to ask her for your direction.'

Katharine's feeling of guilt, overwhelmed for a little while by alarm, returned in full force at these ingenuous words, for bad though it would be to impose on Judith's friends it would be even worse to deceive her brother. Still retaining her grip on the side of the phaeton, she turned her head to look at him, and though his horses were occupying much of his attention he found time to glance at her with a quick, engaging smile. He was a handsome boy, with the same fair curly hair and merry blue eyes as his sister, and was not much older than Katharine herself, having just passed his twenty-first birthday. She felt that she could like him very well, even if he had not been the brother of her dearest friend, and that made the prospect of misleading him even more unwelcome.

'Mr Tillingham,' she said resolutely, 'you are very obliging, but there is something which I must tell you. And I wish you to know that I was unaware of it yesterday when I met you and Judith, and accepted her invitation for the evening.' She hesitated, and then drew a deep breath and added with a rush: 'My uncle, Mr Murrell, keeps a gaming-house!'

Sheer astonishment caused him to drop his hands, so that the horses broke into a canter and Katharine gave a gasp of alarm. He steadied his team after a moment and said in a stunned voice:

'A gaming-house? I don't understand!'

'I do not fully understand myself,' she replied with a hint of bitterness. 'But—but my father's family is not wealthy, and my uncle has chosen this way of making a living. I did not discover it until I returned home from Judith's party last night.'

Edward seemed to have some difficulty in absorbing these facts, for he said in the same bewildered tone: 'But, dash it all, you were at school with Judith!'

'My grandfather, Sir Randolph Storne, caused me to be placed there when my mother died, but that is all he *would* do for me. He does not approve of the Murrells. I dare say Judith has not told you, sir, but I was meant to be a governess. Then a few days ago my uncle came to Medway House and invited me to live with him and his wife in London, and I thought——' She broke off, tears threatening to choke her voice as the magnitude of her disillusionment swept over her again. 'Now it seems that he only wants me here because he thinks I may be of use to him, but I cannot and will not take advantage of the kindness shown me by Judith and her family and friends.'

Edward did not reply to this at once. More experienced than Katharine, he had a much clearer picture than she of the kind of part Duncan Murrell probably intended her to play, but he was still too much shocked by her disclosure to know what comment to make. She, supposing her worst fears to be confirmed by his silence, presently added in a small voice:

'Pray set me down if you wish to, Mr Tillingham! I realize that you would never have invited me to drive with you had you known the truth.'

'Set you down?' he repeated indignantly. 'Well, upon my soul, do you suppose I think any the worse of *you* for what you have just told me? What's more, even if I did, I would not abandon you unattended in the middle of the Park!'

She perceived that she had offended him, and hurriedly begged pardon, but added anxiously: 'You do believe, do you not, that I had no intention of imposing upon Judith's kindness? When I think of the number of people she made known to me I am ready to sink!'

'Oh, come, ma'am, you refine too much upon it,' he assured her. 'It's unfortunate, of course, but I'll wager Judith knows you well enough to realize that you never meant to deceive her. You are in a deuced difficult position, though, there's no denying that! What do you mean to do?'

'There is nothing I can do, Mr Tillingham, except resign myself to the life my uncle designs for me. I have nowhere else to go. No doubt it is my own fault for hankering after pleasures to which I knew I had no right.' She tried to smile as she spoke, but without much success. 'You will explain to Judith, will you not, when next you see her? I mean to write to her, but I shall feel happier if I know that you will add your assurances to mine.'

'You may depend upon that, ma'am, I give you

my word!' he replied firmly. 'As far as Judith's concerned, of course, it will be up to Elsdale to say whether or not you may continue friends, but for myself—well, I hope you don't mean to send *me* about my business?' He saw that she was looking doubtful, and added persuasively: 'Thing is, Miss Murrell, situated as you are, you're bound to feel the need of a friend, and I'd be happy to know you counted me as such. What's more, I'm certain it's what Judith would wish.'

Katharine was still dubious, but then remembered her uncle saying that gentlemen would not hesitate to be upon friendly terms with her even if they would not permit their womenfolk to be likewise. Nor was she trying to deceive Edward in any way. If, being in full possession of the facts, he was still prepared to stand her friend, she could only be grateful for it.

She half believed his words to be no more than a civility, spoken to make her feel more comfortable, but that evening, when at Cassy's command she screwed up enough courage to venture again into the saloons, Edward was there and came instantly to her side. Next morning a large bouquet of spring flowers, accompanied by his card, was brought to her, and that evening he again put in an appearance in the gaming-rooms. Soon he was a regular visitor, and though Katharine was somewhat dismayed at first, fearing that she had unintentionally lured him into becoming a gamester, he assured her with some amusement that if he were not playing in Duncan Murrell's house he would be doing so elsewhere. She was not altogether convinced, but when it became obvious that he came to see her rather than to lose money at the tables she protested no longer.

He was by no means the only man who paid court to her during those first hectic weeks in London, although he was the only one whom she felt she could trust. The gentlemen who patronized Duncan Murrell's house showered her with compliments, and with more tangible tokens of their admiration, so that she soon had a whole drawer full of pretty, expensive trinkets which had been bestowed upon her by various admirers. She was shocked by this at first, and wished to refuse the gifts, but Cassy told her roundly not to be a fool. So she accepted them as graciously as she could, and, because she had all her life been starved of pretty things, could not from time to time resist carrying a dainty fan or wearing some elegant trifle of jewellery.

One of her most persistent admirers was Lord Carforth. There were very few nights when he did not visit St James's Square, and though he gambled heavily—and usually successfully—at the tables, it was plain to everyone that Katharine's presence was the lure which drew him to that gaming-house in preference to any other. Katharine herself disliked him intensely. She had learned to accept with some show of composure the admiration of such men as Jack Ormsby, but to be paid court to by a man of Carforth's age was, to her, deeply repugnant.

It could also have been ridiculous, had Carforth been other than he was, but it was impossible to regard his lordship as a figure of fun. Katharine felt that there was something faintly sinister about him. He had a way of speaking which made the most extravagant compliment sound like a sneer, and she sometimes detected in his eyes an expression which struck her with a tiny chill of fear. He gave the impression of being a man who would enjoy cruelty for its own sake. She sought whenever possible to avoid his company, until Cassy took her sharply to task on that account, paying no heed to her protests and compelling her to accept, and to wear, a pretty and very costly pair of ear-rings which his lordship had sent her. It occurred to Katharine, not for the first time, that Mr and Mrs Murrell were very anxious to please Lord Carforth. Almost they seemed afraid of him.

Edward was angry when she told him of the incident, for he had by this time adopted a possessive attitude towards her and made no secret of the fact that he resented attentions paid to her by any other man. Katharine was both touched and dismayed by this. She had grown fond of Edward and was grateful for his unfailing support, but she knew that Duncan Murrell's niece and Lord Wedgeworth's son and heir could never inhabit the same world. He came to the house almost every night, took her driving, even escorted her and Cassy to a ball, and twice to the theatre, but she could never forget the gulf which yawned between them. On one occasion they came face to face with Lady Ainwood and Fanny, and her ladyship, according Edward the barest and most frigid of nods, ignored his companion altogether. The small incident spoke volumes, and lingered unpleasantly in Katharine's memory.

She had been rather more than a month in London when, on a dull afternoon when Cassy, complaining of the headache, was lying down on her bed, and Katharine absorbed in a novel in the back parlour, the butler informed her that Captain Chard desired to see her, and that he had shown him into the Crimson Saloon. Katharine dropped the book into her lap and stared at him in dismay, conscious of the fact that her heart had begun to beat uncommonly fast. She had been dissuaded by Edward from writing to Judith, he undertaking to set all to rights when the Elsdales returned to town, but there was no one to set matters right for her with Brandon Chard.

'I trust, miss, that I did not do wrong in informing the Captain that you were at home,' Foster added as she did not speak. 'I supposed, since he is Mr Chard's brother——'

'No, you acted quite properly,' Katharine said hastily. 'I will go down.'

Foster bowed and withdrew, and Katharine got up, nervously smoothing her dress and patting her hair. She would have given a great deal to avoid the coming interview, but it was better, perhaps, to see Captain Chard herself than to allow him to hear a spitefully garbled version of the truth from his brother. Whether Bernard was yet aware of Brandon's return to England she did not know. He had never referred to it in her hearing, but she thought it unlikely that Cassy would have been able to keep such a piece of news to herself.

She found Captain Chard standing by the window with his back to the room, but he turned quickly when he heard her come in. She looked anxiously at him as she went forward, but could read no condemnation in his face, only a warm pleasure at seeing her again.

'How do you do, ma'am,' he said, taking the

hand she held out to him, and looking down at her with the smile which she found had lingered with remarkable clarity in her memory. 'I was kept longer in Worcestershire than I expected, but now that I am in town again I have come without delay in the hope of renewing that acquaintance which was so regrettably brief.'

'I am happy to see you, sir,' she replied with difficulty. 'Have—have you only recently returned to London?'

'I arrived last night, ma'am.'

'Then you have not yet seen Mr Tillingham?'

'Edward Tillingham? No, I have not seen him since that evening at the theatre. Is there any reason why I should?'

'Only that he might perhaps have told you something—something concerning me—which I shall now be obliged to tell you myself.' She turned away, twisting her fingers together as she always did in moments of agitation, wondering why it was so much more difficult to disclose the truth to Brandon Chard than to Edward Tillingham. 'You see, sir, this house—that is, my uncle——'

'My dear Miss Murrell,' he interrupted quietly, in a tone of some amusement. 'I have been in far too many gaming-houses not to recognize this one for what it is. There is no need, I assure you, to put yourself in this taking.'

She swung round to face him again, her expression incredulous. 'But are you not excessively shocked?'

He shook his head, the amusement deepening in his eyes. 'It takes a good deal to shock me! I am not even greatly surprised. The location of this house, and my brother's association with it, led me to suspect something of the sort, but I will confess to a certain curiosity as to how a close friend of Lady Elsdale happens to find herself in this situation.'

'I knew you would think that suspicious!' Katharine sank down into a chair by one of the card-tables and covered her face with her hands. 'But do, pray, believe that when I accepted her invitation I had no notion of the truth. I had been in the house barely two days and had never set foot inside these rooms, and, though you will think me excessively stupid, it simply never occurred to me that it was a gaming-house.'

'How should it, indeed?' he replied in a matter-of-fact tone, sitting down on the opposite side of the table. 'Such matters, I believe, are not among those commonly dealt with at a young ladies' seminary. If there *was* any plot behind the events of that evening I am tolerably certain that it was not of your making. Elsdale is a sensible man who will not blame you for something which is no fault of your own, and though I am not very well acquainted with his wife, I do not judge her to be the kind of woman who would condemn an old friend with so little cause.'

This practical point of view was unexpected. She lifted her face, the great violet-blue eyes swimming with tears, and said unsteadily: 'Do you truly believe that, Captain Chard? I know that my friendship with Judith must be at an end, but that would be easier to bear if I could be certain that she still trusts me. Edward—Mr Tillingham—assures me that it must be so, but I cannot rid myself of the feeling that I have imposed, quite unwittingly, upon her charity.'

There was a fractional pause before he said: 'If her brother is prepared to stand your friend—and from what you say I assume that he is—it must surely reassure you on that head.'

'Oh yes, he has been most kind,' Katharine agreed earnestly. 'Indeed, I do not know how I should have gone on these past weeks without his support. I dislike so much being obliged to come into these rooms each evening, though Mrs Murrell says I refine too much upon it, and that what I regard as a want of propriety in the behaviour towards me of some who come here is nothing of the sort, and merely seems so to me because of the strictness of my upbringing.'

There was a faint frown in Brandon's eyes, but he said in the same calm way: 'Does your uncle compel you to come into the gaming-rooms, Miss Murrell?'

'Well, not compel me, precisely,' she replied unhappily, 'but he says that since he has taken the trouble to fetch me from Miss Medway's, and provide me with a home and with pretty clothes to wear, it would be ungrateful in me to refuse to mingle with his guests. I suppose that is true, and that as Mrs Murrell says it *is* better than being a governess, but I fear I shall never be of the smallest use to them. I have not the least aptitude for cards and cannot seem to master even the simplest game, in spite of all they—and your brother also—can do to explain it to me.'

It seemed unlikely to Captain Chard that Mr Murrell had brought his beautiful niece to London merely to assist in his gaming-rooms, but he kept that reflection to himself. He found himself, in fact, in a somewhat awkward situation. The significance of the location of Duncan Murrell's house in a part of London renowned for its clubs and gaming-hells had struck Lord Elsdale quite as forcibly as it had struck the Captain. His lordship knew beyond all doubt that Judith would expect to take Katharine under her wing again as soon as she returned to town, and had taken the precaution of asking his friend to make some discreet inquiries about the Murrell establishment.

Brandon had therefore questioned Lady Elsdale closely concerning her friend—a show of interest which aroused all manner of hopes in her ladyship's heart—and was now as familiar with Katharine's history as Judith herself. This knowledge led him to suppose that, being confronted by a choice between her uncle's gaming-house and a post as a governess, she had chosen the former. He did not even find it particularly blameworthy, save in the deception which she had apparently practised upon Lady Elsdale.

In this frame of mind he had come to call upon her, and that not merely at Elsdale's request, for the memory of her beauty had lingered tantalizingly in his mind all the time he had been away. He had found the house much as he had expected, and Katharine even lovelier than he remembered. What he had not expected was to find her so touchingly innocent, and as completely out of place in this luxuriously appointed hell as Judith herself would have been. It was a discovery which cast an entirely new light on the situation.

'Tell me, Miss Murrell,' he said casually, 'is my brother often in this house?'

'Yes, very often. He assists my uncle in the running of the establishment, and indeed is treated quite as one of the family.' She hesitated, and then added in a low voice: 'I should perhaps tell you, sir, that I am aware of the fact that you and he are not upon the friendliest of terms.'

He looked a little amused. 'Did Bernard tell you so?'

'No, my uncle did. Mr Chard has never referred to you in my hearing, though I think he *must* be aware that you have returned to England.'

'Very probably!' Brandon dismissed the subject of his brother with a slight shrug. 'No doubt we shall meet in due course. Miss Murrell, may I ask a somewhat impertinent question? Do you intend to remain in this house?'

She sighed. 'I have no choice, sir. There are reasons why I cannot return to Medway House, and I have nowhere else to go. That is why I am so very grateful to Mr Tillingham for the kindness he has shown me in spite of my circumstances, and for the assurance that I have at least one friend in London.'

'You are mistaken, Miss Murrell!' Brandon rose to his feet and stood looking down into the lovely face questioningly upturned towards him. This was not what he had expected to say, nor the kind of promise he had intended to make, but the words rose quite naturally to his lips, almost, it seemed, of their own accord. 'You have two friends in London, if you will grant *me* the privilege of counting myself as such. Believe me, I shall be happy to render you any service which lies within my power.'

7

The regular patrons of Duncan Murrell's gaming-house, to whom Bernard Chard was naturally a familiar figure, were that evening astonished to see there another young man so like him in appearance that it was difficult to tell them apart. For this surprise they were indebted to Mrs Murrell. Informed by Maggie that afternoon of Captain Chard's presence, she had been sufficiently curious to forget her headache and hasten down to the saloon. Brandon, who judged that his purpose could best be served by being made free of the house, had exerted himself to please, and Cassy, always susceptible to the attractions of a personable man, was soon assuring him that he would be most welcome at her card-party that evening.

Mr Murrell, when informed of this, was a trifle dubious of the wisdom of risking a public quarrel between the brothers, and took the precaution of dropping a few warning words into Mr Chard's ear. Bernard grinned at him.

'I'll not try to plant him a facer, if that's what you are afraid of. We may detest each other, but we've not come to blows since we were schoolboys. Besides, I'm curious to know what brings him back to England.'

Mr Murrell was not altogether convinced, and when Brandon strolled into the Crimson Saloon that evening, was relieved to see the brothers greet each other with civility, if not with enthusiasm. Bernard's reaction to his twin's arrival was, in fact, far more complaisant than Edward Tillingham's. Edward, who had arrived early and was sitting with Katharine on the sofa at the far end of the room, uttered an exclamation of astonishment and stared at the speaker with an expression compounded equally of annoyance and dismay. When the Captain, having greeted Cassy, came across to join them, he said suspiciously:

'I did not know that you were back in town, Chard! I thought you fixed in Worcestershire for quite some time.'

'My dear Tillingham, I was there for a month, and that was quite long enough, I assure you.' He took the hand which Katharine held out to him, and lifted it briefly to his lips. 'Good evening, Miss Murrell. I trust my presence is not as displeasing to you as it appears to be to Mr Tillingham.'

She laughed, but shook her head. 'You are very welcome, sir, and I am sure that you mistake Mr Tillingham's feelings. He was surprised to see you, that is all.'

Thus prompted, Edward agreed, and made some civil inquiry concerning the Captain's journey. Brandon stayed chatting to them for a minute or two and then moved away to try his luck at the faro-table, and Edward, reverting rapidly to his earlier attitude, said irritably:

'What possessed that fellow to come here? There are plenty of other gaming-houses in London.'

'My dear Edward, why should he not come?' Katharine asked impatiently, for grateful though she was for Edward's friendship she was beginning to be irritated by his possessive attitude. 'He is acquainted with me, and his brother is here constantly.'

He replied sulkily, and in terms so disparaging to Captain Chard that Katharine lost all patience with him. For the first time they came near to quarrelling, and she was so incensed that she even allowed Lord Carforth, who had just arrived, to engage her in conversation. Edward, who loathed his lordship's habit of treating him like a schoolboy, went off in a rage to play hazard in the smaller saloon, and Mr Ormsby, who from a little distance had observed the whole incident with sardonic amusement, said very softly in Cassy's ear:

'The lovely Katharine begins to know her own power! She has just sent young Tillingham about his business.'

Cassy looked round sharply, but when she saw who had taken Edward's place beside Katharine she lifted her plump shoulders in a shrug and turned back to the roulette wheel. Ormsby laughed.

'So she may choose whom she pleases, so long as

he is plump in the pocket,' he remarked. 'How many other golden strings to your bow do you have, I wonder?'

Edward returned to the large saloon in time to take Katharine down to supper, and since his ill-humour had by that time abated she allowed him to do so. She had cherished a faint, secret hope that Captain Chard might seek the favour of her company, but it appeared that his only purpose in coming to St James's Square that night had been to play faro. It was past two o'clock before he rose from the table, the poorer by some three hundred guineas, and signed to a waiter to bring him a glass of wine. As he stood before the fire, sipping this and looking reflectively about him, Bernard sauntered across to join him.

'Your luck seems to be out tonight,' he remarked in a satisfied tone. 'Went down heavily, didn't you?'

Brandon shrugged. 'Three hundred odd, that is all. Nothing to signify.'

'Nothing to signify!' Bernard gave a snort of derisive laughter. 'What, have you made a fortune and come home to spend it?'

'I had a very considerable run of luck in Venice just before I came back,' Brandon replied calmly, 'and have a long way to go before I find myself aground. What a disappointment for you! But, tell me, does your interest in my losses spring from mere brotherly concern, or do you have a financial interest in this delightful establishment?'

'I'm damned if I can see what concern that is of yours,' Bernard replied shortly. 'But, yes, you might say that at least one of my interests in this house is financial.'

THE RELUCTANT ADVENTURESS 101

His brother did not reply at once, but allowed his glance to range over the assembled company. He had been too long absent from London to be familiar with many of those present, but he did not need to know their names to recognize them for what they were. He had seen their like in countless cities in Europe. Hardened gamesters for the most part, with a sprinkling of young, inexperienced men who had obviously been lured to this polite gaming-hell to be fleeced. Mrs Murrell, too, was of a type familiar to him. A handsome woman with a carefully acquired veneer of good breeding which did not quite ring true; a smiling, hard-eyed adventuress who would not hesitate to thrust a young girl along the path which she herself had already trodden.

A faint frown gathered in Brandon's eyes, and his gaze passed from Cassy to a group by one of the small tables on the far side of the room, where Katharine was watching a wager being recorded in the betting-book. Edward stood beside her, one hand on her arm, while on the other side Lord Carforth was making some observation to her, and emphasizing his point by a graceful gesture with his quizzing-glass.

'And your other interest here?' Brandon said softly after a moment. 'No need to tell me what that must be.'

Bernard looked in the same direction and laughed. 'Precisely!' he said. 'Lovely creature, ain't she? But make no mistake, my dear brother, not for the likes of you or me!'

'No?' Brandon spoke carelessly, still watching Katharine. 'For whom, then?'

'Oh, Tillingham, or Carforth, or anyone else rich

enough to pay handsomely for the privilege! Her devoted uncle will set a high price on her, you may depend.'

'Was that his reason for introducing her into this house?'

Bernard was silent for a moment, mockingly studying his brother, and then he laughed again. 'You ask too many questions, Brandon!' he drawled. 'Attend to your own affairs, and leave Murrell and me to attend to ours.'

He sauntered away again, and Captain Chard, having finished his wine, left the house to return to his own lodging in Duke Street. He did not trouble himself to take leave of the company, merely nodding to Cassy as he went past her, and Katharine, surreptitiously observing his departure, stifled a slight feeling of disappointment and put herself out to be pleasant to Edward.

Encouraged by this, he begged leave to take her driving the following day, and after only the briefest hesitation she agreed. He arrived punctually at the appointed hour, and after exchanging a few civilities with Cassy led Katharine out to where a curricle-and-four was waiting in the charge of his groom. The Park, when they reached it, was less crowded than usual, for the sky was overcast and a chilly wind blowing, but in spite of this they had driven only a short way before Edward suggested that they should alight and walk for a little.

Katharine, though faintly surprised, had no objection, and Edward, after assisting her down from the curricle and instructing the groom to walk the horses, proffered his arm and led her along an adjacent path. She had scarcely had time to notice that

THE RELUCTANT ADVENTURESS 103

this was one of the more secluded walks and that they had passed almost immediately out of sight of the carriageway, before Edward halted, seized her hand in both his own, and poured out an impassioned declaration of his love for her.

Katharine was at first as much astonished as she was shocked, for in Edward's company at least she had supposed herself to be quite safe from any improper advances, but surprise was soon overwhelmed by alarm. She did her best to stem the flood of eager words, but her stammered protests seemed only to increase his ardour, and he ended by seizing her in his arms and kissing her. Really frightened now, she struggled frantically until she succeeded in thrusting him away, then, turning, fled back the way they had come.

He caught her just as she reached the promenade, and she struck wildly at his hand as it closed on her arm. She was still almost beside herself with fright, and careless of anyone who might see them.

'Kathy, wait!' Edward's face was pale now, his voice unsteady. 'I am sorry! I did not mean to frighten you, but you are so beautiful——'

'Take me home!' she interrupted in a shaking voice. 'Take me home this instant! Oh, how could you? What have I ever done to lead you to suppose——?' She broke off, and covered her face with her hands.

'Kathy, for God's sake!' he said urgently. 'I will take you home, I will do anything you wish, only don't create a scene here, there's a good girl! I was wrong, but I swear I meant no harm! Kathy, there is a carriage coming, and ten to one it is somebody who knows us.'

The dismay in his voice recalled to her the impropriety of being discovered in such a situation, and helped her to regain command of herself. Shaking off his grasp, she straightened her hat with trembling hands and turned to walk towards the curricle, while a landaulet occupied by a haughty dowager swept disdainfully past. The groom, his countenance schooled to an expression of wooden vacancy, helped her up into the carriage, and for the whole of the short journey back to St James's Square she sat rigidly erect, staring straight before her. Only when her uncle's house was reached did she speak, and then she said in a stifled voice:

'Do not get down, Edward. It is not in the least necessary.'

He started to protest, but, as the groom had already jumped down and was waiting to assist Miss Murrell to alight, the protest was not attended to. She ran quickly up the steps without a backward glance, and he realized that to follow her would do more harm than good. Waiting only to see her safely admitted to the house, he drove off, silently cursing his inept handling of the situation.

As luck would have it Cassy was in the hall when Foster opened the door to Katharine, and one glance at the girl's face told her that something untoward had happened. She had a shrewd suspicion what it might be, but made no comment and merely accompanied Katharine to her bedchamber, where she inquired solicitously what had disturbed her. Katharine, thoroughly overwrought, poured out the whole story, and Cassy listened with a show of sympathy which might have surprised some who knew her. She agreed that Edward's conduct had been very shocking, but added that it would not do to refine too much upon it.

'It is my fault for allowing you to be so much in his company,' she said, 'but I supposed he was to be trusted not to go beyond what is proper. But do not hold it too much against him, love! You are very beautiful, and gentlemen sometimes find it difficult to control their feelings.'

'I can never face him again, never!' Katharine declared tragically. 'Do not ask me to go into the saloons tonight, Cassy, for he is certain to be there, and I shall be ready to sink! Oh, I am so ashamed!'

'Nonsense!' Mrs Murrell replied bracingly. 'It will not do to be brooding over what has happened. Of course you must come down, but I promise that Edward shall not vex you, and you need do no more than bid him good evening. In fact, it will be a very good thing to let him see how much he has offended you.'

'Yes, but if he tries to talk to me I shall not know how to avoid it. It is no use pretending otherwise, Cassy, for you know I have not the least notion how to give anyone a set-down.'

'Then he shall be given no chance to talk to you,' Cassy reassured her. 'Your uncle and I will be on the watch for him, and I'll drop a word in Bernard's ear besides. Now don't fret, my dear, and don't cry any more, for pity's sake! You will only make yourself look a fright.'

Katharine remained unconvinced, but she had already learned that it was worse than useless to argue with Cassy. So that evening when Edward, hiding certain doubts under an assured manner, came into the Crimson Saloon, he found Katharine there indeed, but with three or four gentlemen grouped around her. Nor did she, for once, appear to have any inclination to escape from her admirers. She greeted him civilly enough, but immediately turned again to her companions, leaving him no choice but to occupy himself elsewhere until she should be disengaged.

This he did by wandering disconsolately about the room, pausing by this group or that, watching the spin of the roulette wheel or the fall of the cards at faro, and all the while casting surreptitious glances in her direction. At last the gentlemen drifted away, but though Edward moved at once towards Katharine Bernard was there before him, and remained blandly impervious to all hints to take himself off.

Edward began to grow annoyed, but did his best to conceal it. He did not like Bernard Chard, and had no intention of allowing him the satisfaction of making him lose his temper. He had hopes of persuading Katharine to go down to supper with him, but before he could find an opportunity of asking her, Brandon rose from one of the small tables, where he had been playing picquet, and forestalled him. Katharine accepted without hesitation and went off on the Captain's arm, while Edward glared after them and Bernard regarded him with undisguised amusement.

'I should try my hand at faro if I were you, Tillingham,' he advised him mockingly, 'for you know the old adage. It looks to me as though you should be devilish lucky at cards tonight.'

In the supper-room Brandon found a seat for Katharine at a small table by the wall, fetched her some food and some iced champagne, and then sat down opposite to her and said with a smile:

'I must count myself very fortunate, for I am sure that I am at this moment the most envied man in the room.' He lifted his glass to her. 'Your very good health, Kate!'

She looked startled. 'I was not aware, sir, that I had given you leave to use my name.'

The smile broadened, and an eyebrow was quizzically lifted. 'I have heard you called Katharine by half a dozen different men, so surely I may call you Kate? To my mind, it suits you better.'

'I think I would rather be Katharine,' she said doubtfully. 'No one has ever called me Kate before.'

'Then they should have done! "Bonny Kate. The prettiest Kate in Christendom." Do you not know your Shakespeare?'

She regarded him curiously. 'I do, sir,' she replied frankly, 'but I had not supposed that *you* would be familiar with the plays. I hope, though, that you do not think me a shrew?'

'I think you . . .' He paused for a fraction of a second, and then continued easily: 'I think you are disturbed about something tonight, Kate. You remember, I trust, that I asked leave to be counted as your friend?'

'Thank you. I do remember, and I am grateful for it, but as for my being disturbed tonight—well, perhaps I am a little, but it is something quite trivial, I assure you.'

He was not disposed to believe her. He had observed her careful avoidance of Edward's company, the relief in her eyes when he forestalled the younger man in taking her to supper, and was able to hazard a fairly accurate guess at what had occurred, but it was plain that she had no intention of confiding in him. She began to speak at once of his journey to Worcestershire, asking him in a rallying tone if he had truly found his stay there as tedious as he pretended.

'For surely,' she added, 'you must have found a great deal to do at your home after so long an absence?'

He laughed and shook his head. 'Not in the least! I have a first-rate agent, you know, who is devoted to my interests and keeps everything in excellent order, and all goes as well when I am away from the place as when I am there. Sometimes I think it goes better!'

'Tell me about it,' she said suddenly. 'Your home, I mean. What is it like?'

'Do you really wish to know,' he asked with some amusement, 'or are you merely endeavouring to make polite conversation?'

'I would like to know,' she replied gravely. 'You seem to care nothing for it, and your brother begrudges you the possession of it. I cannot help wondering what sort of place it is.'

'Well, Mallows is no ancient castle or stately mansion, I assure you. Just an old manor-house, not particularly large or handsome, with old-fashioned gardens around it, and a small park. A couple of farms, a handful of cottages, and that is the full sum of it. The countryside is fruitful and pleasant without being in any way remarkable, and most of the house has been shut up since my mother died five years ago. Not in the least impressive, you will agree. Yet it would not be entirely true to say that I care nothing for it. No doubt I shall be content to end my days there when I grow too old to find any pleasure in a roving life, and I would never allow it to fall into decay, but at present the mere thought of such an existence fills me with the most profound dismay.' He paused, studying her face with its wide, grave eyes and wistful mouth, and then asked gently: 'What are you thinking, Kate?'

She sighed. 'How strange it is that you, owning so pleasant a place, cannot bear to live there, while I . . .' She shrugged, and smiled a little, though her expression was still wistful. 'Perhaps the thought of a home is most precious to those who have none.'

Before he could reply, Bernard, who had followed them into the supper-room and had for several minutes been watching them from a little distance, lounged across to join them. When he spoke his tone was jesting, but there was curiosity in his dark eyes as he looked from one to the other, and even a hint of suspicion.

'Devil take it, what ails the pair of you? You have faces long enough for a funeral!' He did not wait for an answer, but put down the glass he was holding and dragged forward another chair. Sitting down astride it, his arms folded upon its back, he regarded his companions mockingly, plainly delighted at having found an excuse to intrude.

'We were merely indulging in a little rational conversation,' Brandon replied calmly. 'But your mention of funerals sets me in mind of a trifle of family news I heard while I was at Mallows. Old Jasper Crawthorne died two months ago.'

'What, the old miser dead at last?' Bernard exclaimed. He was silent for a second or two, and then added with a chuckle: 'Well, you're not looking so glum on his account, I'll wager! Most people have been wishing him underground for years.'

Brandon laughed, but then, glancing at Katharine, saw that she was looking distinctly shocked. 'You should not look for any proper sentiments in us, Kate,' he told her, 'but not even the most upright character could in honesty mourn for Cousin Jasper. He was the most tyrannical old curmudgeon it has ever been my misfortune to meet.'

'Queer in his attic,' Bernard added dispassionately. 'Lived in a confounded ruin of a house right out in the wilds, with a high wall all round it, the gates always locked at sunset, and a devilish great brute of a dog roaming about the whole time. Like something out of one of those damned silly novels you females are always reading.'

'True enough,' Brandon agreed as Katharine directed an incredulous glance towards him. 'The fact is, of course, that he should have been put under lock and key years ago.'

'Cousin Emma must be giving thanks he's slipped his moorings at last,' Bernard said idly, and turned a somewhat malicious look upon his brother. 'Going to try your fortune with her again, Brandon, now the old man's not there to put a stop to it? No need for an elopement this time! You can put up the banns, all right and tight!'

Katharine, directing a startled and unconsciously dismayed look towards the Captain, saw a quick frown descend upon his brow. He said impatiently: 'You know damned well there was never any question of an elopement! When I was there seven years ago Emma was little better than a slave to that old villain. Her brother had been turned out of doors, and I persuaded her that she would be far happier at Mallows, with our mother, than in her grandfather's house. I was going to escort her there, but she took fright at the last moment, and refused to leave.'

'That's not the way I heard it,' Bernard retorted with a grin, 'and not the way Cousin Emma regarded it, I'll wager! Surely you're not going to disappoint her after all these years? She cannot be much above three-and-thirty, and her grandfather's money-bags will make up for what she lacks in looks.'

'You are as much out in that supposition as in all the rest,' Brandon said contemptuously. 'There never was any truth in the tales of old Crawthorne being a miser. I know he was always in mortal fear of being robbed, but that was merely one of his crazy delusions. The truth is that he had nothing worth stealing! In fact I hear from his lawyer that Emma finds herself in such reduced circumstances that she is obliged to sell the house.'

Bernard checked in the act of raising his glass to his lips. 'Sell the house?' he repeated blankly.

'Certainly! It would cost far more than she can afford to make it habitable, and in any event it is a great deal too large for her. She hopes to realize enough from the sale to purchase a small cottage in a less isolated position.'

Bernard sipped his wine thoughtfully. 'You've seen her, I suppose?'

'No, I had my information from the lawyer. I visited the house on my way back to town, but Emma was indisposed and could not receive me. It is scarcely surprising! I gather that the old man was bedridden for several months before he died and needed constant nursing. He would have no one but Emma to tend him.'

'Sort of thing he would do!' Bernard finished the wine and put down the empty glass. 'I'd have been tempted to poison the old devil if I'd been in her place. Damn it all, I've a good mind to post down to see her! Dare say she'd be glad to see me! After all, we're her only relations, and I *was* her brother Freddy's closest friend.'

'Scarcely worth the trouble, Bernard!' There was a satirical note in Brandon's voice. 'I assure you she has not two halfpennies to rub together! But if you do go I warn you that you will be obliged to put up at the nearest inn, for Emma's notions of propriety have not altered in the least, and will not permit her to have a bachelor staying beneath her roof. That, at least, was the answer which was conveyed to me when I offered to remain to give her any help which she might need with her grandfather's affairs.'

Bernard stared at him for a moment and then burst out laughing. 'Good God, does she flatter herself to that extent? Must be as dicked in the nob as the old man!' He pulled out his watch, glanced at it, and rose to his feet. 'I must go upstairs! I promised Cassy I'd take her place at the roulette table at one o'clock, and it's already ten minutes past. Dare say she's in the fiend's own temper by now!'

8

Mrs Murrell was indeed growing increasingly impatient, but when Bernard at length strolled unhurriedly up to the roulette table she made no comment but merely cast him one angry glance. As soon as he had taken her place she turned to Edward, who had been gambling recklessly and with varying fortune on the spin of the wheel, and requested him to take her down to supper. He did so with a marked lack of enthusiasm, and having settled her in the supper-room, supplied her needs, and provided himself with a glass of wine, showed a decided tendency to let his attention wander to the table where Katharine still sat with Brandon Chard. Apparently the Captain had succeeded in restoring her spirits, for she was laughing merrily at something he had said. Edward stared at them in moody abstraction until at last Cassy said bluntly:

'Small use glowering across the room in that sullen fashion! After what happened this afternoon it's not to be wondered at that she prefers any company to yours.'

He looked startled, and then shamefaced. 'She told you?'

'Told me?' she retorted. 'I asked her! Not that there was the least need, for when a girl goes out driving with a man, and returns in the state of agitation Katharine was in, it's plain enough what has happened. God save us, Edward! What possessed you to do such a thing?'

He flushed. 'I could not help it—though I did not mean to frighten her. Dash it all, ma'am, you know how it is——'

'Yes,' she interrupted impatiently, '*I* know how it is, but then I am not an innocent miss fresh from the schoolroom! Katharine may live in a gaming-house now, but she was brought up in exactly the same way as your own sister, and was as much shocked as she would have been at being treated in such a fashion. If you had the least degree of common sense you would have realized that such was bound to be the case.'

He tossed off the rest of his wine with a defiant gesture and signed to a waiter to bring him another glass. When this had been done he said sulkily: 'Perhaps so, but the harm's done now! What I want to know is how to repair it.'

Cassy shrugged, and picked up her knife and fork again. 'You must beg her pardon.'

'I know that!' he replied irritably. 'Why the deuce do you suppose I came tonight? But I cannot beg her pardon when she will not let me come near her.'

'Well, *I* cannot force her to listen to you! You may be sure that I have done my best to convince her that it is all a misunderstanding, but she will pay no heed. Perhaps your sister can intercede for you when she returns to town. Katharine might listen to her.'

'But confound it all! That may not be for weeks!' Edward's voice was charged with dismay, and he shot another anxious glance towards Katharine, who was now leaving the supper-room on Brandon's arm. The Captain's head was bent a little towards his fair companion as he spoke to her, and, though Katharine's eyes were demurely downcast, a little smile was hovering about her lips and she was plainly quite at ease in his company. More at ease, in fact, than she had ever seemed with anyone, Edward included.

'And in the meantime,' Cassy remarked, completing Edward's remark for him, 'there's no lack of rivals to take your place—and most of them a deal too experienced to put her in a fright as you have done! Look at her now, for example! And she has not met Brandon Chard above three or four times.'

Edward muttered under his breath something extremely uncomplimentary to Captain Chard, and then asked, more audibly, what Mrs Murrell advised him to do. Mrs Murrell gave the matter her consideration.

'You'd best write to her,' she said at length. 'I will undertake to see that she reads the letter, and after that she may consent to receive you again. The thing is that the silly child has taken into her head that you were making her a dishonourable proposal this afternoon——'

'No!' There was no mistaking the sincerity of Edward's dismay. He had flushed like a schoolboy, and was stammering in his eagerness to assure Cassy of her mistake. 'Mrs Murrell, I swear it was no such thing! I want to marry her!'

An expression of satisfaction, which Edward was too perturbed to notice, passed fleetingly across Cassy's face. She said in a matter-of-fact tone: 'Well, it seems you forgot to tell her so, and I'm sure it's no wonder she read quite a different meaning into your behaviour. What else was she to think, reared as she has been? You may depend that she expects any proposal of marriage to be preceded by an application to her uncle for leave to address her.'

He looked up eagerly. 'Perhaps I could speak to Mr Murrell now!'

'My dear boy, you cannot make such a request of him in the middle of a card-party! Besides, you must know you need look for no opposition from him, for if Katharine is agreeable there is nothing we should like better than to see her become your wife. But if you take my advice you will make your peace with her before doing anything else. Write to her, as I suggested, and I dare say that by this time tomorrow everything will be in a fair way to being settled.'

In this assumption, however, Mrs Murrell proved to be guilty of undue optimism. Edward's letter, sentimentally enshrined in a basket of red roses, was brought to Katharine while she and Cassy sat at breakfast. She lifted it rather doubtfully from its fragrant resting-place and spread out the crackling sheets of paper, while Cassy, ostensibly occupied with her own correspondence, surreptitiously watched her. The letter was a long one—it had, in fact, taken Edward most of the night to compose—but it did not seem to arouse in Katharine those feelings of gratification and delight proper to a young lady receiving her first and very flattering proposal of marriage. She read it with an expression of gathering dismay, and then sat with it in her lap, staring blankly before her, for so long that at last Cassy was obliged to prompt her a little.

'Does Edward write to beg your pardon, love? A basket of red roses, too! I must say that was a very pretty gesture.'

'Cassy!' Katharine transferred her troubled gaze to the other woman's face. 'He wishes to marry me!'

Cassy beamed at her. 'There, child, did I not tell you that you were making a great deal too much fuss about what happened yesterday? To be sure, he should have spoken to your uncle first, but a young man in love does not always consider such things. This is splendid news! I wonder if your uncle has yet gone out? He should be told of this at once.'

'Cassy, you do not understand!' Katharine's strained voice broke in upon these transports. 'Edward wishes me to marry him secretly.'

'Secretly?' A slightly anxious note crept into Cassy's voice. 'You mean an elopement?'

'No! Oh no, nothing as shocking as that! He says'—she looked again at the letter—'that if I will do him the honour of accepting him he will obtain a special licence so that we can be married quietly and without any delay. And that he has reason to believe that his offer will meet with no opposition from my uncle or from you.'

'Well, that's true enough, at all events!' Cassy said bluntly. 'A fine pair of fools we should be to raise objections to so splendid a match. *I see no harm in doing as he suggests!* To be sure, you would prefer to have a grand wedding, I dare say, with bridesmaids and a lace veil and all the rest, but I'll tell you to your head, my dear, that your uncle's in no position just at present to incur such an expense. Time enough for cutting a dash once you are married.'

'You do not understand!' Katharine exclaimed despairingly. '*I* know why Edward desires a secret wedding, even though he does not say so! It is because of his father. Lord Wedgeworth could not possibly approve of such a match.'

'Well,' Cassy admitted cautiously, 'I dare say he might be a trifle put out, just at first, for there's no denying, love, that people such as the Tillinghams expect a girl to have a handsome marriage-portion, though why they should do so, rich as they are, is more than I can understand. But once he makes your acquaintance he will see that there can be no reasonable objection to your marrying Edward.'

'No reasonable objection?' Katharine repeated incredulously. 'His heir to marry a woman without a penny to her name, whose own grandfather will not acknowledge her existence, and whose uncle—forgive me, Cassy, but it is the truth, after all—is the proprietor of a gaming-house? You think Lord Wedgeworth would accept *that* with complaisance?'

'Once you are married he will have to accept it. Edward is of age and free to marry whom he chooses, and his lordship has nothing to say to the matter.'

'Has he not?' Katharine's voice was bitter. 'Sons have been disinherited for less, and even if it did not come to that it would be bound to result in a permanent estrangement between him and Edward. Lord Wedgeworth feels very strongly upon such matters. I remember Judith telling me of the commotion which was created when his sister, who was a widow and turned forty years of age, decided to marry a gentleman whom Lord Wedgeworth felt was not worthy of her. She did marry him, but his lordship has neither seen her nor spoken of her from that day to this. And the gentleman in question owned a small estate and a competence of a thousand pounds a year.'

'Upon my word!' Cassy thrust back her chair and jumped to her feet to pace angrily about the room. 'I do not understand you, Katharine! I tell you that once you are Edward's wife his lordship will have nothing to say to the matter. What if he does refuse to accept you at first? He will soon change his tune when you present him with a lusty grandson to carry on the family name!' She watched with exasperation the blush which mounted to Katharine's cheeks, and struck her hands together in a fury. 'God save us, this is no time to be missish! Edward adores you, and I supposed that you felt a decided partiality for him.'

'I like him very well,' Katharine replied in a low voice, 'but even if I felt the strongest romantic attachment for him I still would not consent to a clandestine marriage. I could not so betray him, or my friendship for Judith. You have no right to expect it of me! My mother's suffering and humiliation, my own unhappy circumstances, are the direct result of just such a match as the one you now urge upon me. I will never accept Edward's offer!'

From this decision nothing could shift her, not Cassy's arguments, nor Mr Murrell's, nor even Edward's, when he came, later that day, for his answer. He was bewildered and dismayed, and even Cassy, to whom he turned for advice, could suggest nothing more helpful than that he should continue his courtship in the hope of eventually persuading Katharine to change her mind.

This he proceeded most assiduously to do. He sent her flowers and presents, wrote her impassioned letters, and was so often at the house that Bernard asked caustically if he had taken up residence there. Katharine's steadfast refusal to marry him he would not accept, and she was not permitted to refuse the invitations he showered upon her. He took her driving, dispensing with the attendance of a groom so that he might be free to plead with her; to Vauxhall Gardens, newly opened for the summer; and even to such unlikely places as Westminster Abbey and the Tower of London, since she had once expressed a wish to see these historic landmarks. She began to be almost afraid that sheer persistence would wear down her determination, and could only be thankful his sister was still delayed in Wales. She knew that she could expect no support from Judith, who would be more likely to add her urgings to Edward's, and feared that she would be unable to hold out against them both.

She formed the habit when Edward was present in the gaming-rooms of avoiding his company or, if that proved impossible, of encouraging others to join them. This rarely presented any difficulty, but it was somewhat to Katharine's surprise that she found Bernard more than willing to abet her, for she had expected him to be of the same opinion as her uncle and Cassy. She was grateful, but could not entirely overcome her earlier mistrust of him.

Where his brother was concerned she made no such mental reservations. Captain Chard had come to occupy an increasingly prominent place in her thoughts, a fact which troubled her a little. He was a frequent visitor in St James's Square, gambling heavily and accepting both gains and losses so calmly that anyone who did not know the truth would have supposed him to be immensely wealthy. He was popular with the other men, and flirted expertly with Cassy as well as with Katharine herself. Mrs Murrell was plainly intrigued, and took an early opportunity of questioning Bernard concerning his brother.

Katharine was present during this conversation, to which she listened with an eagerness which she hoped was not apparent to her companions, and learned enough about the Captain to realize that her first impression of him had been a correct one. Brandon Chard was an adventurer in the most literal sense of the word. The long years of military campaigning had exactly suited his reckless temperament, and peace inspired in him no wish for a more settled way of life. He roamed from one country to another as the fancy took him or adventure beckoned, and gambled with his life as readily and light-heartedly as he gambled with gold. He was, in fact, exactly the sort of man whom Katharine had all her life been taught to distrust and despise, but this knowledge, it seemed, had no effect on the erratic behaviour of her heart, which still tended to leap absurdly whenever she saw him, and grow heavy with disappointment when he did not appear.

One evening, when the saloons were somewhat thin of company, and those present intent upon serious gambling rather than idle conversation, Katherine was less successful than usual in fending off Edward's attempts to talk to her alone. Cassy had gone downstairs to deal with some minor crisis in the supper-room, so that Bernard was presiding over the roulette table, and Katharine could see no one else in the room likely to come to her rescue. Then Edward's attention was claimed for a moment by the arrival of a friend of Lord Elsdale, who wished to know when his lordship might be expected in London, and she seized her opportunity to slip into the smaller saloon. This was occupied only by a group of gentlemen silently intent upon deep basset, and she was able to seek refuge in a small and seldom-used anteroom beyond, intending to remain there until the other rooms had filled up a little.

Hardly had she sat down, however, when the sound of the opening door brought her swiftly to her feet again, vexed and dismayed by the failure of her ruse, but it was not Edward who had discovered her. Jack Ormsby, his dark face already a little flushed with wine, was triumphantly regarding her from the doorway.

'Hiding, my dear?' he remarked, coming in and closing the door behind him. 'Or have you come to keep an assignation? What a curst ungrateful fellow, whoever he may be, to keep such beauty waiting.'

Katharine, ignoring this pleasantry, moved

quickly towards the door, for Edward's company was infinitely preferable to Ormsby's, but he moved as swiftly to bar her way. She found herself trapped between his outstretched arm and a tall Chinese cabinet which stood against the wall, and looked up at him in alarm. He laughed, and moved closer.

'Always try to avoid me, don't you?' he said with a sneer. 'Has that vixen Cassy warned you off? Pay no heed to her shrewish tongue, my dear! She'll have told you a pack of lies, I'll wager, as you'll learn when you become better acquainted with me.'

The door quietly opened again as he spoke. Brandon's voice said ironically: 'A prospect which Miss Murrell, I am sure, finds as disagreeable as I do. You would be much wiser, believe me, to bestow your attentions in that quarter where they are likely to be welcomed.'

Katharine gave a thankful gasp, and Ormsby swore and spun round. His face was dark with fury and his fists clenched, so that for an instant she feared that he was about to fling himself upon the intruder. Brandon had stepped aside and was holding the door open in a meaning way; he looked faintly amused, but there was something in his face, in the slight, inquiring lift of one quizzical brow, which made Mr Ormsby think better of offering any physical violence. He muttered something under his breath and strode out of the room.

Brandon closed the door behind him and strolled across to Katharine, looking humorously at her flushed and troubled face. She cast him one fleeting glance and then turned her head away, saying in a stifled voice:

'Thank Heaven you came in, but oh, what must

you be thinking? He followed me in here—indeed, I had no notion that he would . . .'

Brandon took her firmly by the elbow and guided her to a chair. 'Sit down, Kate, and compose yourself!' he said with some amusement. 'No dark suspicions have leapt into my mind, I assure you. I came in by way of the small saloon just in time to catch a glimpse of you entering this room. Then Ormsby followed you, and I judged it prudent to follow Ormsby. As I had just passed Edward Tillingham on the stairs, looking exceedingly put out, I had no great difficulty in guessing the reason for your retreat.' He paused for a second, and then added in the same light tone: 'Has that young cub been pestering you also?'

'Oh no!' She looked up quickly, anxious to dispel any misunderstanding. 'At least, not in the same way. It is just that he *will* persist in asking me to marry him.'

His brows shot up in astonishment and for a second or two he did not speak. Then he said casually: 'Am I to understand that the prospect does not appeal to you?'

She hesitated for a moment, but the chance to discuss her predicament with a sympathetic listener was a temptation too great to resist. Almost before she realized it she was pouring out the whole story of Edward's desire for a secret marriage, the pressure which was being put upon her to agree, and her own determination not to do so.

'For even if I wished to marry Edward,' she concluded, 'I could not bring myself so to come between him and his father. Why, it would be the shabbiest trick to serve him, when I know so well—

and he does not—how disastrous such a marriage can be. But my uncle and Cassy say that is all nonsense, and that Lord Wedgeworth would be bound to accept me once I was Edward's wife.'

'Yes, I'll warrant they do!' Brandon's tone was sardonic. 'They will be telling you next that it is your duty to marry him.'

'They *have* told me so,' she replied despondently. 'They plague me and pester me until it is beyond all bearing. I do not wish to be disobliging, but I *will* not be persuaded into doing anything which I know to be wrong.'

He looked as though he were about to say something, but thought better of it. There was silence for a space, while Katharine absently opened and shut the fan of silk and ivory which hung from a ribbon about her wrist, and Brandon stood gripping the back of a chair and frowning as though in deep thought. At last he said abruptly:

'Do you recall the night we first took supper together, and you asked me about my home?'

She looked up, faintly surprised. 'I recall it very well. You made it sound delightful.'

He nodded. 'You would find it so, I think, and at Mallows you would be spared both young Tillingham's importunities and the unpleasant attentions of such fellows as Ormsby. I believe you might be happy there.' He paused, studying her troubled face and wide, startled eyes, and then laughed softly. 'Don't look so alarmed, Kate! No doubt I am being very clumsy, but bear with me, I beg! This is the first proposal of marriage I have ever made.'

She continued to stare at him, unable to speak, scarcely able to believe that she had heard him correctly. If Edward's proposal had astonished her, Brandon's took her breath away, the more so because she realized, with a blinding flash of revelation, that it was the only one she would ever wish to accept. Her happiness was so unexpected, so overwhelming, that at first she felt almost stunned by it, and before she could collect her wits sufficiently to reply he went on:

'I am not a rich man, but in spite of all my gambling and adventuring my inheritance, such as it is, has never suffered. I can offer you a home and a comfortable independence, and as my wife you would be completely free of Murrell and of whatever plans he may be making for you. Nor need you fear that you would be plagued by my presence, for I have not spent more than a few weeks at Mallows during the past ten years. I am a restless fellow, as no doubt you know, and expect soon to be off on my travels again.'

The words were as unexpected as a douche of cold water, and after the first shock had the same steadying effect. Pity, chivalry—she did not know which had prompted his proposal, but one thing at least was certain. It was not love for her. She needed a moment or two to gain command over her voice, but then she said in a tolerably steady tone:

'No doubt I am being excessively stupid, but I do not perfectly understand what you are offering me.'

'My home, and the protection of my name,' he said quietly. 'Did I not make that clear?'

She nodded, looking down at the fan now gripped tightly between her hands. The brief dream of happiness had faded as soon as it flowered, and dignity was all she had left. It seemed suddenly very precious.

'Yes, but I was so surprised. I had no expectation . . .' She paused, drew a deep breath, and nerved herself to look up into his face. 'I am deeply grateful, and—and deeply honoured, but it would not answer, you know. And I am tolerably certain that my uncle would never permit it.'

'Very likely!' There was a hint of grimness in Brandon's voice. 'But what applies to Lord Wedgeworth would apply even more certainly to him. He would be obliged to accept it, once the marriage had taken place—and that could very easily be contrived.'

She shook her head, not looking at him, and rose to her feet. She knew that she could not endure much more. 'I cannot accept your offer, sir, but I shall always most gratefully remember it, and—and feel the warmest regard for you. Now I think I had better go back to the saloon.'

'I see what it is,' he said ruefully. 'I have spoken too frankly. Would you have preferred me to imitate Tillingham's romantic outpourings, or perhaps Ormsby's more forceful approach? Believe me, Kate, either would be very easy—and very dishonest!' He was standing close beside her now, and when she looked up at him she saw that his face was pale, with a rigid look about it as though he were holding his emotions ruthlessly in check. 'It would be a lie to say that I am indifferent to you,' he went on in a low voice. 'No man, I think, could fail to be stirred by such beauty as yours. I could make you all manner of promises, but I am sufficiently well acquainted with myself to know that no woman, however beautiful, could keep me for long content with the life of a country squire, and I'll not seek to trick you by pretending otherwise. I respect you enough, Kate, to wish to deal honestly with you.'

'I understand,' she whispered, 'and I thank you for it, and . . . for everything.'

She moved away from him towards the door, and he went at once to open it for her, but paused, grasping the handle to look down into her face. He was smiling now, rather wryly, but she knew that he still spoke in all seriousness.

'There is, of course, an alternative. You could come adventuring with me.' He paused inquiringly, but when she did not speak he laughed, softly and ruefully. 'I thought not! You do not really approve of me, do you, Kate? But I was never more in earnest in my life, and even though you will not marry me, remember that upon my friendship you may always depend.'

9

On the following morning Katharine sat alone in the parlour. She had declined an invitation to accompany Cassy in a search for a particular shade of ribbon to trim a new bonnet, and the sewing which she had brought down from her bedchamber lay neglected in her lap. Chin on hand, she sat staring into the fire which a late spell of cold weather had made necessary, and wondering, as she had wondered for most of a sleepless night, whether she had been intolerably foolish to refuse Brandon Chard. He had offered her a great deal more than, situated as she was, she had any right to expect; more, she realized, than she was ever likely to be offered again. She thought of the old manor-house he had once described to her, and knew that it was just such a home as she had always longed for. She would be secure and peaceful there, even though she might be lonely. Could she not content herself with that?

Her meditations were presently interrupted by Foster, who came in with a letter and the information that the bearer now waited below for Miss Murrell's reply. With a sinking heart she recognized Edward's handwriting, and dismissed the butler, saying that she would ring for him when her answer was ready.

She expected to find another lengthy avowal of Edward's devotion, but, though the burden of the letter was much the same as that of all its predecessors, it was couched in terms of far greater urgency. He had just received news, Edward wrote, that his father was expected in London that evening, having travelled all the way from the family estates in Norfolk for the express purpose of seeing his heir. As Lord Wedgeworth commonly lived all the year round in the country and had the greatest possible dislike of town life, only a matter of the most grave urgency could have brought him to London, and there was no doubt what this might be. There was no time now to obtain a special licence, but if they set out immediately they could be well on their way to Gretna Green before his lordship learned of their departure.

Katharine's first emotion on reading the letter was a profound relief. Lord Wedgeworth's presence in town would mean the end of Edward's ardent courtship, and she hoped that his lordship would be grateful to her for refusing to be won over. Then, hard upon the heels of relief, dismay came rushing. There were many hours still to pass before Wedgeworth's arrival, and there was every likelihood that her uncle and Cassy would discover the altered situation, from Edward if not from herself. So determined upon the marriage had they proved themselves that Katharine almost believed them capable of bundling her by force into a carriage with him and sending her off to Scotland, willing or not.

She sat clutching the letter and wondering rather desperately what to do, so intent upon the problem that when the door opened it took her by surprise. She gave a fightened gasp and tried to thrust the letter out of sight behind her as Bernard came in, and his eyes brightened with curiosity and malice. Treading briskly across the room, he grasped her wrist and twitched the crumpled letter from her fingers, ignoring her cry of protest. She sprang up and tried to recover it, but he laughed and fended her off with one hand while he read rapidly through it. A low whistle escaped his lips and he grinned expectantly at her.

'Gretna Green, eh?' he remarked. 'So it's to be a race for the Border, with Papa in hot pursuit! That will be an original touch to the affair, at all events. Usually it's the bride's father who does the chasing.'

'You know very well that I would never consent to such a thing,' Katharine replied crossly, abandoning the attempt to recover her property, 'and Edward should know it, too! If I would not agree to marry him from this house, in my uncle's presence, I will certainly not agree to anything as shockingly vulgar as an elopement.'

Bernard leaned his arms on the back of a chair, the letter dangling carelessly from his fingers, and shook his head at her in mock reproach.

'You, my girl, are an improvident little prude,' he told her impudently. 'Only consider for a moment! This is your last chance of becoming a viscountess one day, and you are prepared to whistle it down the wind. Not that you'll be allowed to, of course! Duncan and Cassy will see to that.'

'You will not tell them?' Katharine's voice was sharp with dismay. 'Bernard, I beg of you, do not!'

'Lord, my dear, there'll be no need! They have only to set foot inside the front door to see Tillingham's man waiting impatiently to carry your answer back to him.'

'Oh dear, I had forgotten that!' She sank down into her chair again, pressing her hands distractedly to her cheeks. 'And if I send a refusal Edward is certain to come himself to try to persuade me, and that will be even worse. Oh, what am I to do? I am so afraid that they will find some way of compelling me to go to Scotland with him, and then I shall be obliged to marry him.'

Bernard regarded her in some perplexity. 'Damme if ever I saw a woman so set against an advantageous marriage,' he said wonderingly. 'It's not as though Tillingham were old or ill-favoured, either! Take my advice, my dear girl, and settle for the young spark. You might do a great deal worse.'

'No, I will not, and I did not think that *you* would urge me to do so,' she replied reproachfully. 'You have always seemed willing enough to help me when I try to avoid being left alone with him.'

He continued to study her, tapping the letter idly against the back of the chair, an expression in his face which she could not interpret. A faint smile hovered about his usually sullen mouth, but there was a calculating look in his eyes.

'Since you're so determined against it,' he said at last, 'I might help you, if I felt so inclined. I could go to Tillingham and tell him it was all a plot to trap him into marriage, and that you were in it from the first. That it was your reason for coming to London, and that once the knot's safely tied you mean to lead him a merry dance. He's a jealous young devil, so it shouldn't be hard to convince him of that.'

Katharine considered the suggestion with some repugnance, for she could not like the prospect of being presented to Judith's brother, and so eventually to Judith herself, in so unfavourable a light. Bernard's unexpected offer of help she passed over with scarcely a second thought. It seemed merely one more chance for him to stir up the sort of mischief in which his malicious nature delighted.

'He would not believe it,' she objected at length. 'If that had been my purpose I would have married him long since.'

'Oh, I'll think of some reason to account for it! You'd be surprised how ingenious I can be when I set my mind to it. Well, do you want to try it? Duncan or Cassy may come in at any moment, and in any event I have more amusing things to do than to stand prosing here.'

Katharine came to an abrupt decision. 'Yes,' she said recklessly, 'we *will* try it, and if you succeed I shall be exceedingly grateful.'

'That's more than Duncan and Cassy will be,' he retorted. 'They've been gloating over the prospect of battening on Tillingham for the rest of their lives.' He screwed the letter into a ball and tossed it into her lap. 'Best burn that right away, and I'll send Tillingham's man about his business on my way out.'

He sauntered from the room, and Katharine,

casting the letter into the fire, sat watching it until it crumbled into flakes of ash, and wishing that all her problems could be as easily disposed of. She could not feel easy, and after a few minutes got up to wander restlessly about the house. She went into the Crimson Saloon and stood for a while looking from the window, and then drifted downstairs and peeped into her uncle's study at the back of the house. He spent a good deal of time there during the day, but to her relief the room was empty and the big writing-desk shut.

Returning to the parlour, she sat down and began to turn the pages of a periodical in a desultory fashion. A glance at the clock told her that Bernard had been gone for well over an hour, and she was just wondering how much more of this suspense she would be able to bear when she heard his footstep on the stairs, and a moment later he came into the room.

'Tillingham insisted on coming back with me,' he said in answer to her anxious question. 'Said he wouldn't believe it unless he heard it from you. Now don't put yourself in a pucker,' for Katharine had uttered an exclamation of alarm. 'You need say only that everything I told him was true. I'll come with you—he's waiting in the Crimson Saloon—but we'd best make haste. If Cassy or Duncan come in while he's here there'll be the devil to pay.'

Thus urged, she accompanied him in some trepidation downstairs and into the saloon. Edward was standing in the middle of the room, his gaze fixed with painful intensity on the door, and as she entered he moved a step nearer to her and then halted again. Bernard took Katharine's cold hand in his and drew it through the crook of his arm and held it there. Leading her forward, he said mockingly:

'Now, Tillingham, though you were obliging enough to call *me* a liar to my face, I hope you will be less discourteous to Katharine. Tell him, my dear!'

'Kathy, it isn't true?' Edward's voice shook a little in spite of all his efforts to steady it. 'For God's sake, tell me it is not!'

'It is perfectly true, Edward,' she replied steadily. 'Everything that Bernard told you. I am sorry.'

He stared at her for a moment in silence, his face as white as his neckcloth, and then with an inarticulate exclamation he brushed past them and out of the room. They heard his hasty footsteps descending the stairs, and then the crash of the front door slamming behind him. Bernard released Katharine's hand and made her a mocking bow.

'The *coup de grâce!*' he said with a grin. 'Only you could have dealt it, my dear, but I fancy that we have now seen the last of your troublesome suitor.'

'Poor Edward!' she whispered. 'He looked so shocked! I hate being obliged to hurt him so.'

'He'll recover,' Bernard said callously. 'Dare say he'll even thank us for it some day, when he's less green than he is now. And don't you forget, my girl, whom you have to thank for ridding you of him. You may have a chance to repay me one day!'

Edward did not appear in the gaming-rooms that night, to Cassy's vehemently expressed surprise. Bernard, overhearing her, glanced at Katharine with an almost imperceptible wink, but she was still haunted by the memory of Edward's white, stricken face and turned quickly away. Brandon looked in for an hour or so, but she had no chance to do more than exchange a few commonplace civilities with him, and indeed felt a considerable degree of embarrassment in his company.

On the following night, when Edward was once again absent, Cassy's surprise began to be tinged with uneasiness, and even the imperturbable Mr Murrell had a faint frown between his brows. Katharine, lacking both Edward's persistent pursuit and Brandon's support—for Captain Chard did not visit the house that night—was forced to spend a large part of the time in Lord Carforth's company, and was thankful when the last guest had departed.

Later that same morning the blow fell. Katharine, who had agreed to go with Cassy to Bond Street, was coming down the stairs towards the hall when Bernard was admitted to the house. He carried a folded newspaper in his hand, and when he caught sight of her came quickly up the stairs to meet her. There was a look of suppressed amusement in his face, but he said nothing and merely held the paper out to her, pointing to a certain spot on the page. Katharine looked, and then gasped with astonishment, for the item thus indicated was an announcement of the engagement of Edward Tillingham to Fanny Ainwood.

Cassy, joining them at that moment, read it, and let out a shriek that fetched Mr Murrell from his study. All thought of going out was instantly abandoned and the four of them went upstairs again to the parlour, Cassy loudly condemning Edward, and the perfidy which had prompted him to court two young ladies at the same time. Katharine's attempt to justify his action in the light of her own refusal to marry him merely diverted this storm of abuse on to her own head, until she was quite dazed by the epithets such as ungrateful, improvident, and selfish, which were heaped upon her. She might, when Cassy eventually paused for breath, have said more, but caught Bernard's warning glance and thought better of it. To reveal the deception they had practised upon Edward would benefit no one.

Mr Murrell was less vociferous than his wife, but Katharine was left in no doubt of the extent of his anger, and only the knowledge of having done right enabled her to face him with any degree of composure. He pointed out to her, briefly and coldly, the folly of playing fast and loose with the most eligible suitor she was ever likely to have, a folly which had now brought its inevitable reward, and added that she would oblige him in future by paying more heed to his wishes. Left alone at last, Katharine relieved her feelings by a prolonged bout of weeping, and felt more strongly tempted than before to turn to the one remaining person who seemed to care anything at all for her happiness.

Brandon did not put in an appearance at St James's Square that night, but on the following morning, when Cassy, who still could scarcely bring herself to speak civilly to Katharine, had left the younger woman at home alone, Foster brought word that Captain Chard had called to see her. With a sudden lifting of her spirits, she thanked him and ran eagerly downstairs to the Crimson Saloon.

Brandon was waiting for her very much as Edward had waited a few days before, and at sight of his face the words of greeting died on her lips. She had not thought it possible for him to look so stern, and his glance flicked over her with a cold contempt that frightened her.

'What is it?' she faltered. 'Why do you look at me so?'

'You need to ask?' The words were flung at her in a tone that matched the look in his eyes. 'I have just left Edward Tillingham. He told me everything. No doubt you imagine that you have been very clever?'

Katharine moved abruptly to the nearest chair and sat down. It had never occurred to her that Brandon would discover the means she had used to put an end to Edward's wooing unless she confessed it to him herself, and the shock seemed temporarily to have scattered her wits. She said faintly:

'It had to be done. There was no other way.'

'Good God, are you completely heartless?' he asked angrily. 'It may surprise you to know that when I chanced to meet that boy in the early hours of this morning he was three parts drunk, and talking quite seriously of putting a period to his existence. And if he had done so, *you* would have been as much responsible as though you had yourself put a bullet into his brain.'

'That is unjust!' Katharine's voice was trembling with shock and anger. 'Nor do I believe that he had any such intention, whatever he may have said to you. My treatment of him can scarcely have dealt him so severe a blow as that, since he lost so little time in offering for Miss Ainwood.'

Brandon regarded her for a moment in silence, his expression compounded strangely of scorn and astonishment. 'Do you know,' he said at length, 'you are almost unbelievable? For all your own damnable treachery, you can still be jealous of that unfortunate girl.'

'I am not jealous of her! I think she and Edward may suit very well, and I wish them both happy. I do not deny that I deceived him a little, but I do not see why that should make *you* so out-of-reason angry.'

'Deceived him a little!' he repeated. 'Oh, my God!' He came to rest his hands on the table by which she sat, leaning across it towards her. 'Kate, let us have done with pretence! It was a very ingenious plot, I'll grant you that! The carefully arranged chance meeting with Lady Elsdale, the confession to Edward that your uncle kept a gaming-house, the pose of persecuted innocence which was bound to arouse all his most chivalrous instincts. I own it puzzled me a little at first that you did not succumb to the lure of being "my lady" one day, and marry him secretly as he wanted you to do, but then I found the answer to that in your own history. You feared that Lord Wedgeworth might follow your grandfather's example, and disinherit Edward if he married a wench out of a gaming-hell. This way the profit may be smaller, but at least it seems certain.'

Katharine pressed her hands to her head. The bitter, scornful words seemed to pound against her brain, making only partial sense, and she was too hurt and bewildered to unravel their meaning. She could think of nothing but his contemptuous, hostile eyes, and the coldly furious voice that seemed to cut her like a whip.

'In fact the whole plan would have succeeded to admiration,' he continued, 'but for one chance which you could not possibly foresee. I mean the chance of my return to England, and my friendship with Elsdale—and, of course, the fact that I too was deceived by you! Does that amuse you, Kate? I am sure it must amuse Bernard. It could afford him little satisfaction to fool a callow boy like Tillingham, but to fool me . . . ! And that I even went so far as to offer you marriage must be, to him, the most exquisite jest of all.'

She lifted her stricken face towards him with an incoherent murmur of denial, and put out her hands in a little, pleading gesture. He broke off abruptly and after staring down at her for an instant turned sharply away, saying in a hard voice:

'Well, no matter for that! It is a folly which is over and done with, but if you think that I will stand idly by and watch you cheat the Tillinghams out of a fortune you are sadly out in your reckoning. For Lady Elsdale's sake, and Miss Ainwood's, if for nothing else, I must do my utmost to prevent it.'

'I think one of us must be mad!' she said despairingly. 'I do not know what you are talking about.'

He cast her an impatient glance. 'Abandon that pose of innocence, Kate, I beg of you. You do it supremely well, but I am beginning to find it irritating. You will be trying to tell me next that your uncle has not demanded ten thousand pounds from Edward Tillingham as the price of the letters which he was foolish enough to write to you—at Cassy's suggestion, of course!'

She stared at him, and said in a stunned voice: 'Ten thousand pounds?'

'The figure surprises you? I own it is excessive, but then the young fool played directly into your hands by announcing his engagement to Miss Ainwood. But you expected that, did you not? It seems it was common knowledge that he was on the point of offering for her when you introduced yourself to his notice.'

'I did nothing of the kind, and in any event how could I have known such a thing? I was not even in London.'

'No, but your uncle and Cassy were, and Bernard, and a piece of gossip of that nature is easily picked up from the sort of company that frequents this place.'

Katharine made a determined effort to regain command of herself. It was plain now that there was more trickery afoot than she had even suspected, and that Brandon supposed her to be implicated in it, but the truth would never be reached by hurling insults at each other. She rose to her feet and faced him, saying as calmly as she could:

'Let me properly understand this, if you please. You say that my uncle offers to sell Edward his own letters for ten thousand pounds?'

'I do! Oh, he does not put it quite like that, of course. He merely informs him that you intend to bring a suit for breach of promise against him, using the letters as evidence, and that ten thousand is the price you will set upon your . . . disappointment. In fact he knows very well—you all know it—that Lord Wedgeworth would never permit such a case to come into court. The scandal would be too great.'

She stared at him, her first numb horror giving

way to a rising anger. 'And you? *You* dare to believe me capable of that?'

'I begin to believe you capable of anything, but you have miscalculated a little, for *I* intend to take a hand in the affair. I shall see Lord Wedgeworth and persuade him to refuse this preposterous demand. Bring your case, Kate! Let us have the whole sordid business dragged into court, and I swear I will expose the whole pack of you for the scoundrels you are. Murrell and his wife are as smooth a pair of tricksters it has ever been my privilege to meet. My brother is a rogue—I can prove that a dozen times over! And you, my bonny Kate? I do not think your role of wronged innocence will be very convincing once the whole truth is made known. You overreached yourself a trifle when you allowed Bernard to disclose to Edward the fact that for the past year you have been his mistress.'

For one stunned instant she continued to stare at him, and then her hand shot out in an instinctive, outraged reaction to that intolerable insult, and struck him hard across the face. He recoiled a little, but looked at her with an even greater degree of icy contempt than before.

'You are out of character, Kate,' he said in a voice that bit like acid. 'The schoolroom miss you pretend to be would have swooned with horror at such an accusation. No, do not put yourself to the trouble of denying it! Remember that you have already admitted its truth to Edward.'

The words brought her up short, changing her anger to despair as she realized how Bernard had tricked her, how completely she was enmeshed in

THE RELUCTANT ADVENTURESS 143

the web of lies and treachery that he and her uncle and Cassy had spun around her. And Brandon believed it. He had not even tried to discover how far she was involved, whether she was in fact as much a victim of the plot as Edward himself, but had condemned her unheard out of his own wounded pride. Anger and desolation possessed her, but she saw clearly that there was one thing which must be done before she could give way to the tide of misery welling up within her.

'Wait!' she said briefly, and ran from the room and up the stairs to her bedchamber, where she had left Edward's letters—she recalled bitterly how Cassy had laughingly urged her to cherish them—hidden among her gloves and handkerchiefs. She dragged open the drawer and then stood stockstill, frozen with horror, for the bundle of letters had gone.

Although she knew it to be useless she rummaged frantically through the drawer, tossing its contents wildly about, and then through the next, and the next. Then she turned and went slowly back to the saloon.

'The letters have gone,' she said dully. 'Someone has taken them from my room.'

He laughed shortly, on a note of disbelief which spurred her to further action. If her uncle had taken the letters, and she had no doubt that he had, she could think of only one place where they were likely to be. She turned and hurried from the room again, and this time went down the stairs to the hall. She knew that Duncan had gone out some time before, and had no hesitation in going to his study. The big bureau was closed but not locked, and when she flung it open a bewildering array of drawers and pigeon-holes confronted her.

She cast a considering glance over them, discarded the pigeon-holes as unlikely, and turned her attention instead to the drawers. All but one opened at her touch, and a brief search through them yielded nothing. The last drawer was locked, and there was no sign of the key.

She was aware that Brandon had followed her into the room and was watching her with impatient contempt, as though he considered her anxiety to be assumed and her efforts to repair the harm merely a pose for his benefit. She tried the drawer again, rattling it to and fro, and then her glance fell upon an antique dagger, which Mr Murrell used as a paper-knife, lying on top of the bureau. Recklessly snatching it up, and inserting the blade into the slit at the top of the drawer, she wrenched at the hilt with both hands, aware as she did so that Brandon had taken a quick, startled pace towards her. There was a sound of splintering wood, and the little drawer slid open.

There were a number of papers inside, but Katharine had eyes only for a bundle tied together with a narrow ribbon. Picking it up, she glanced quickly through its contents and then turned, holding it out to Brandon.

'There are the letters!' she said furiously. 'All except the last, and that I burned. Take them to Edward, and tell him that no power on earth will ever persuade me to make use of the promises they hold.'

He took them as though scarcely aware of what he did. His expression had changed. There was perplexity in his eyes as he looked from the letters to the splintered drawer, and then to the girl standing white-faced and defiant before him. He said uncertainly: 'Kate...'

'Why do you stay?' Her voice shook with the strain of the past half-hour, but there was a blazing anger in her eyes. 'I am everything that is vile, capable of any infamy! Have you not proved that to your own satisfaction? Now go, and I hope I may never be obliged to set eyes on you again!'

He hesitated for a moment, as though there were something he would like to say, but then he shrugged and turned away, thrusting the letters into his pocket. Katharine stood rigid while his footsteps receded from her across the hall, but when the front door had closed with a sound of finality behind him she gave a gasp and dropped into the chair before the desk, burying her face in her hands.

10

The storm which had greeted the announcement of Edward's betrothal was as nothing to that which broke about Katharine's head when she confessed to returning the letters to him. After Brandon's departure she had closed the desk and gone slowly upstairs to her own room, too distressed by what had passed between them to give any thought to the inevitable reckoning. It was only when she heard Cassy's voice on the landing, issuing some instruction to Maggie, that fear of the consequences of her impulsive action awoke within her. Cassy did not come in search of her, but after some time a heavier footfall on the stairs, mounting with urgent haste, told her that her uncle had returned.

She had been sitting all this while on the edge of the bed, her hands gripping the counterpane on either side of her, and her eyes staring vacantly at the opposite wall. She had not wept. The shock had been too great, the wound too deep, for tears. She heard Mr Murrell go into his wife's dressing-room and for a minute or two there was a faint, confused murmur of voices. Then the door opened again and he called angrily:

'Katharine! Katharine, come here! Immediately!'

She rose slowly to her feet, her movements stiff and mechanical. She would have given a great deal not to obey the summons, but her limbs moved slowly, as though against her will, and carried her across the room and out on to the landing. Duncan Murrell was standing in the open doorway of Cassy's dressing-room. He watched her walk towards him, stood aside for her to enter, and then followed her into the room and closed the door.

Cassy was standing in the middle of the floor, her eyes narrowed and her mouth set in a thin, hard line, but at first she said nothing. It was Murrell who spoke, his voice cold and even.

'Katharine, while I have been out of the house, my desk has been broken open and certain papers taken from it. Foster tells me that Brandon Chard has been here. Will you be good enough to explain?'

'I took the letters,' Katharine said in a low voice. 'Captain Chard told me of the demand you had made. I found the letters and gave them to him and told him to return them to Edward.'

'You had the temerity to rifle my desk while my back was turned?'

Her uncle's accusing tone struck a sudden spark of anger from her. 'You had the temerity to steal them from my room! Those letters were mine! You had no right to touch them.'

Cassy laughed, a harsh, sneering sound with no amusement in it. 'Perhaps you think the profit should be yours also. That we have no right to that, either!'

'I never thought of profit! Had I guessed your wicked purpose in urging me to keep them I would have burned them long ago, and I thank God I was informed of the truth in time to prevent it.'

'You may find less cause for thankfulness when all is said and done,' Cassy snapped, and rounded suddenly upon her husband. 'Well, Duncan? Did I not warn you at the outset that no good would come of bringing your precious niece here? Twice within a week she has tossed away a fortune, and that after all the money you have spent on her. God save us, you ought to take a whip to her, to teach her who calls the tune in this house!'

'Nothing,' Mr Murrell replied cuttingly, 'would give me greater satisfaction, but apart from relieving our feelings it would do no good at all.'

'Tell me what will!' she retorted, flinging herself into a chair and drumming her fingers angrily against its arm. 'We are in worse case now than we ever were.'

He shook his head, still studying Katharine with a thin-lipped smile. 'Oh, I think not, my love! Our hope of rich profit may have disappeared, but there still remains a way out of our most pressing difficulties. It is not what we originally intended, but it will serve well enough.'

For a few seconds she continued to frown at him, and then her brow cleared and she laughed, her glance turning with malicious satisfaction towards Katharine.

'So there is, to be sure,' she said with a sneer, 'and this time we'll see to it that nothing goes amiss, even though our fine lady here may not care for the prospect. It will have to be Carforth.'

'Lord Carforth?' Astonishment and dismay jerked the name from Katharine's lips. 'Good God! You cannot expect me to marry *him*!'

'We do not expect it!' Murrell spoke quietly, but in a tone that struck her with sudden fear. 'For one thing, Lady Carforth still enjoys excellent health, and for another, his lordship, even if he were free, is not fool enough to offer marriage to a young woman in *your* situation. Only a romantically minded boy like Edward Tillingham would consider so much to be necessary.'

For a moment longer Katharine stared at him, uncomprehendingly, and then his meaning struck her with stunning force. She went white, and said in a shaken whisper: 'I will not! Oh, how could you even think of such a thing?'

'You will do as you are told,' he said flatly, 'for I am so deep in debt that unless I make a recovery soon we shall all find ourselves in the Fleet. Lord Carforth is my principal creditor. If I can settle with him, the worst of my troubles will be over—and he is prepared to cancel the debts if you become his mistress. And that, my child, is precisely what you are going to do.'

'No!' Katharine spoke in a whisper between white lips. 'I hate him! I would die rather than let him touch me!'

Cassy laughed stridently, and Mr Murrell shook his head. 'That is not the choice before you, Katharine. It is Carforth or a debtors' prison, and you will, I think, find his lordship to be the lesser of two evils.'

'He will set you up in a very pretty establishment,' Cassy added mockingly, 'for he's always generous to a woman living under his protection. I dare say you *would* prefer one of the young bucks who have been casting out lures to you, but let me tell you, my girl, that Carforth's wealth is more important than any fancy you may have for a handsome face. More important to us, at all events!'

With a cry of disgust and despair Katharine turned and fled back to her own room. She understood now, clearly and for the first time, the heartless manner in which her uncle had tricked her. To him she was nothing, a mere tool to be used to rescue him from his difficulties, and forgotten when she could be of no further use. Twice she had overset his plans, and she would be given no opportunity to do so a third time. He and Cassy would be constantly on their guard, and would stop at nothing to force her into a dishonourable alliance with Carforth. Yet against what, after all, did they need to keep watch? There was no way of escape, no one now who would lift a finger to save her.

In this frame of mind she was found at length by Bernard. A stealthy tap on the door heralded his arrival, but when she made no response he opened the door a little way and thrust his head into the room. Katharine, who was lying prone on the bed, started up on to her elbow and said in a low, frightened voice:

'Go away! How dare you come into my room! If you do not go at once I shall call to Cassy.'

'Oh, don't start screeching, for God's sake!' he

said softly in a tone of disgust, and coming farther into the room, closed the door and leaned his shoulders against it. 'This is a fine to-do you have caused, damme if it isn't! What the devil possessed you to do such a thing?'

'If you cannot see that for yourself, *I* could never explain it to you,' she said wearily, getting up from the bed and smoothing her crumpled dress. 'And if you came just to ask me that, I wish you will go away again. I have enough to bear without you being found here.'

'I won't be found! Duncan and Cassy are still dressing. As to why I am here, I've come to help you.'

'As you helped me the other day, no doubt?' she said bitterly. 'Oh, how *could* you have told Edward such a thing about me—about us?'

He grinned. 'Had to find some way of accounting for your refusal to marry him, didn't I?' He paused, eyeing her shrewdly. It was growing dark in the room, but enough light remained for him to see her face. 'Are you sure it's not brother Brandon's opinion you're concerned about, rather than young Tillingham's? You and he have been mighty close just lately.'

She turned quickly away, hoping that she had not betrayed how close to the truth his words came, concentrating on her dislike of him in an effort to forget for a moment the aching sense of loneliness and loss.

'Oh, do go away, Bernard!' she said drearily. 'You will find no amusement in baiting me, I assure you.'

'Very well, I'll go, but if you want to avoid becoming old Carforth's bit of muslin I can tell you how to do it—and you would be rid of Duncan and Cassy into the bargain. I'll be in the anteroom behind the small saloon as soon as the first guests have arrived.'

He did not wait for a reply, but opened the door and retreated as stealthily as he had come, leaving Katharine staring after him. She could never trust him, yet so desperate was her situation that she knew she must hear what he had to say, and waited impatiently for the evening's gamesters to arrive. Bernard was waiting for her in the anteroom when she slipped in from the saloon, and a faint stab of vexation went through her at his calm certainty that she would come.

'Knew you'd not be able to resist hearing what I have to say,' he greeted her with a grin. 'If there's one thing that never fails it's a woman's curiosity!'

'Curiosity did not bring me,' she replied indignantly. 'I am just so desperate that I can afford to neglect no offer of help—even one which comes from you.'

He laughed. 'Don't bare your claws at me, my dear! We are not here to quarrel.'

He pulled forward a chair for her and another for himself, sitting down close beside her and leaning forward to speak in a low voice which did not carry far.

'Do you remember one night at supper,' he asked abruptly, 'when Brandon spoke of a cousin of ours who recently died, old Jasper Crawthorne?'

She nodded. 'I remember. You both said he was mad.'

'So he was, but what's more important he was also a miser. There's a fortune hidden in that tumbledown old house of his, if only we can lay hands on it.'

Katharine stared at him, disappointment and vexation struggling for mastery in her expression. 'I suppose you consider this a famous jest,' she said bitterly. 'To trick me into coming here to listen to a pack of nonsense. Your brother said there was no truth in the tales of the old gentleman being a miser.'

'Much he knows of it! Listen, Katharine, old Jasper's grandson was a crony of mine, and I had this story from him. He told me one night when he was three parts disguised. It seems that years ago, when everyone was expecting Bonaparte to invade us, Jasper had the notion of turning all his money and property into jewels, so that he could hide it from the French if ever they got here. The danger passed, but by that time the idea was fixed in his mind that everyone was trying to rob him, and he went on buying jewels and hiding them away with the rest. He sold all his land except for the house he lived in, and wouldn't spend a penny. He lived like a pauper, and made Freddy and Emma do the same. Their parents were dead, you see, and Jasper was their guardian. When Freddy found out about the jewels—came on the old man rubbing his hands over 'em one night—he was kicked out of the house and told never to come back. He came to London, and that's when we began to see a good deal of each other. Freddy was willing enough to bide his time, you see. The old man couldn't last for ever!'

Katharine, her interest caught in spite of herself, regarded him with a frown. 'Then why has he not yet claimed his grandfather's estate?'

'Because he died a couple of years ago. Poor Freddy! The one thing he didn't bargain for was that the brandy would finish him before the old man slipped *his* moorings. It's plain Emma knows nothing of the jewels. You heard Brandon say she means to sell the house.'

'You ought to tell her,' Katharine said doubtfully. 'But I do not see what all this has to do with me.'

'I'm coming to that! The jewels are hidden somewhere in that house, but I don't know where, and if I'm to find them I'll have to stay in the confounded place for a few days. No use trying to get in unbeknown, for what with the locked gates and the dog and one thing and another, one might as well try to break into a fortress. I mean to pay Emma a visit, but you heard what Brandon said! She's got such devilish strait-laced notions she won't have an unmarried man staying in the house. But if you came with me, posing as my wife, she'd have no objection at all.'

Katharine stared at him, her prime emotion one of complete astonishment, but this was quickly followed by anger. She said indignantly: 'It would be bare-faced robbery! What right have you to suppose that I would help you in anything so dishonest?'

'Because you'd be helping yourself at the same time. I shall be very much surprised if there's less than fifty thousand pounds' worth of jewels in old Jasper's strongbox, and there may be a great deal more. Cousin Emma would not know what to do with half such a sum! She'll be quite happy in her little country cottage, busying herself with good works, but you and I, Katharine—that's a very different matter.'

Katharine shook her head, but without much conviction. She was shocked to discover that she could consider, even for a moment, Bernard's preposterous suggestion, and knew that it was a measure of her own desperation that she did so.

'It would still be robbery,' she said wretchedly. 'Those jewels belong to your cousin, and we should be stealing them from her.'

'If we don't, I'll lay odds someone else will. She would never have the sense to keep quiet about them, and some smooth-tongued adventurer would persuade her into marrying him. It would be the easiest thing in the world.'

'In that event,' Katharine said tartly, 'I wonder you do not do so yourself.'

He laughed and possessed himself of her hand, sliding his other arm round her shoulders. 'A damned fool I should be to tie myself to an old maid who's as plain as a pudding, when with a little ingenuity I might have the jewels *and* a lovely creature like you!'

'Yes, you are very ingenious, are you not?' she said bitterly, holding herself rigid within the encircling arm. 'You proved that with the lies you told Edward. I suppose you hatched this scheme as soon as you heard that I had given back his letters, and that my uncle had now no hope of settling his debts to Lord Carforth.'

'Oh, before that, my dear girl, before that!' he replied airily. 'I planned it as soon as you refused to elope with Tillingham, for I knew then that you'd be faced before long with the prospect of becoming old Carforth's property. Don't tell me you're simple enough to suppose that even if Duncan had got the ten thousand from Tillingham he would have wasted any of it on settling with Carforth, when the old man's more than willing to take you instead?' He read his answer in her sudden pallor and wide, horrified eyes, and laughed again. 'Good God, you did believe it! What an innocent you are!'

Katharine pulled herself from his grasp and jumped to her feet, moving blindly away to the window. The long curtains had not yet been drawn across it, and against the darkness beyond the glass acted like a mirror, so that she could see a shadowy reflection of the room behind her. Bernard had also risen to move slowly towards her, and, seen thus dimly, it might have been Brandon himself who paused close behind her. Katharine closed her eyes as a sharp stab of pain went through her. So alike in looks, so different in every other way. If only some miracle could now set the one brother in the other's place.

'Well, Katharine?' Even their voices were alike when Bernard spoke without his usual mocking drawl. 'You loathe Carforth, and you've never tried to hide it, and he's not the man to forgive a slight of that nature!' He put his hands on her shoulders and spoke softly, his lips close to her ear. 'With me life could be very different! Think what we could do with fifty thousand and more! No need to stay in England. Paris, Rome, Vienna—we could see them all.'

'Come adventuring with me.' Another voice echoed faintly in Katharine's ears, waking a passionate regret that she had paid no heed to its plea. She said uncertainly, seeking to delay a little longer the moment of decision:

'Where does your cousin live?'

'Oh, in Gloucestershire, beyond Stow-on-the-Wold. It's a devilish bleak and outlandish spot, but with any luck we can be there by nightfall.' His hands on her shoulders turned her round to face him. His voice, still low, vibrated with suppressed excitement. 'Will you come, Katharine?'

'I will come!' She spoke flatly, not looking at him. 'At least, I will if I can escape from this house unobserved, though I do not know how that is to be contrived.'

'*I* know!' he said triumphantly. 'Got it all planned!' He let her go and moved away into the middle of the room. 'Make an opportunity during the evening to slip away and pack what you'll need, and leave the portmanteau or whatever it is in your room. I'll find some way to smuggle it out of the house while Duncan and Cassy are engaged in the saloons. Then if you *are* seen going out in the morning, no one will know you don't mean to return. Look out for old Maggie, though! She's as shrewd as the devil, and she'd do anything for Cassy.'

'Suppose my uncle follows us?'

'How can he? He may guess we've gone together, but he doesn't even know of the Crawthornes' existence. Once you're away from the house you'll have nothing to fear from him.'

She nodded without speaking. One part of her mind was intent upon the plan of escape, but another part seemed to be watching with utter detachment and marvelling at what she meant to do. She had no illusions concerning the nature of the bargain she was making. It filled her with dread and self-disgust, but the alternative she could not bring herself to face.

'At ten o'clock then! I'll have a chaise-and-four waiting at the corner of King Street.' He held out his hand to her, and like a sleepwalker she went towards him and put her own into it. 'Slip out unobserved if you can! The longer they think you still in the house, the better!'

She nodded again, and, still wrapped in that frozen detachment, made no resistance when he took her in his arms. She did not recoil from his kiss, but neither did she respond, and after a moment he let her go, looking at her with a faint, puzzled frown.

'You'd best go back to the saloons before Cassy misses you,' he said abruptly. 'I'll wait here a little so that she does not see us together.'

Obediently she went to the door, and finding herself unobserved, stepped out into the small saloon. The rest of the evening passed for her in a kind of daze, but when at last all the guests had gone, and she went wearily up to bed, the portmanteau which she had packed and left just inside her room had gone, and she knew that the first part of the plan had been accomplished.

The second part proved to be almost absurdly easy. Shortly before ten o'clock Katharine left her bedchamber and went quietly, but with as confident a manner as she could contrive, down the stairs. The voices of servants reached her from the saloons, but she encountered no one, and was able to let herself out into the street without anyone being aware of her departure. A few minutes later she was seated beside Bernard in a post-chaise which threaded its way through the traffic in the direction of Hyde Park Corner.

They spoke little until they were free of the town, but when the busy streets were behind them Bernard took her left hand in his and pulled off her glove. Then he took a ring from his pocket and slid it on to the third finger.

'A damned good thing I thought of this!' he remarked. 'Emma would think it devilish odd if my wife wasn't wearing a wedding-ring.'

Katharine looked down at the gold band encircling her finger, and her eyes filled with sudden tears. She turned her head quickly away, but not before Bernard had seen them and laughed softly.

The journey was both tedious and exhausting, for, in spite of his assurance that they would not be followed, he showed no inclination to linger on the road. He seemed wholly preoccupied with plans for finding the jewels, and in racking his brains to recall details of a house which he had not visited for years, and then only briefly. Katharine, who had been in dread of amorous advances, seized thankfully on this reprieve and entered into the discussion as far as she was able.

She was too sick at heart to pay much heed to the countryside through which they passed, but toward evening she could not help noticing that a subtle change had come over the landscape around them. The flat Oxfordshire plain was left behind, and the road climbed steadily into a land of rolling hills and sudden, winding valleys. Hedges had given way to low stone walls, and every building was of stone also, grey in the grey dusk. The wind, which had been rising steadily all the afternoon, swept ruthlessly across the high crests of the hills, driving grey clouds before it and penetrating coldly even into the closed chaise. A harsh, unfriendly place the Cotswold country seemed to Katharine from that first glimpse of it in the dull and chilly twilight.

Darkness fell before they reached their destination, but at length a few gleams of light from cottage windows indicated that they were passing through a village, which Bernard said was only a couple of miles from his cousin's house. The village lay sheltered in a fold of the hills, but after a mile or so the road began to climb again.

'Not far now, thank the Lord!' he remarked with satisfaction. 'The house is about halfway up this hill.' He paused, listening to the roar of the wind through the trees beneath which the chaise was now passing. 'And of all god-forsaken spots to live in, this is the worst I've ever encountered! No wonder old Jasper went mad.'

He broke off, for the chaise had lurched to a stop and showed no disposition to move forward again. After a little, Bernard let down a window and thrust out his head to shout an irritable question. An indistinguishable answer from the post-boy reached Katharine's ears, and Bernard swore and opened the door.

'He says there's a damned great branch across the road,' he informed Katharine. 'I shall have to help him to shift it.'

He jumped down into the road and Katharine huddled in the corner of the chaise, rubbing her hands together to try to warm them. She was tired and chilled, and, now that the journey was almost over, in the grip of a rising panic. What was she doing here, alone with Bernard Chard in this unfriendly countryside, committed irrevocably to him and to his dishonest schemes?

At last the door of the chaise opened and he took his place again beside her. 'It's beginning to rain,' he informed her as the carriage moved forward. 'A good thing we're nearly there.'

She agreed in a subdued voice, and sensed rather than saw that he was looking intently at her. After a moment he moved closer and put his arm around her, pulling her against him.

'Poor little Katharine!' he said caressingly. 'It's been a devilish long journey, hasn't it, my love?'

'Do not! Oh, please, do not!' The panic she felt sounded in her voice as she pulled herself free and retreated as far as the narrow confines of the chaise allowed. 'Oh, how I wish I had not come!'

There was a moment of silence, and then he said in an odd tone: 'A trifle late in the day, my dear, to be having second thoughts!'

'I know that!' She had not meant to betray her feelings, knowing instinctively that any show of regret or fear would merely provoke him, but by now she was too tired and frightened to dissimulate. 'Oh, why should I be persecuted by men like you and my uncle? I must have been mad to agree to pose as your wife, and I wish I were dead!'

He made no reply, nor did he try to touch her again. The chaise crawled up the long hill behind its labouring horses while Katharine tried to compose herself, wiping away the tears which had filled her eyes and endeavouring to subdue a rising tide of hysteria which made her want to scream aloud.

There was another lengthy halt when the gates of Emma Crawthorne's house were reached, for these were locked, and it was no easy task to persuade the old man who at last emerged from a tumbledown lodge to open them. Bernard was obliged to alight again before he could convince the ancient of his identity, but at last the gates were opened and the chaise jolted forward over the uneven surface of a badly kept drive.

When Katharine was at last handed down from the carriage she could see nothing but the tall gables and chimneys of the house outlined against the hurrying, faintly luminous clouds. The wind whipped her skirts about her ankles and tugged at her bonnet, so that she gasped for breath and was thankful when Bernard drew her into the shelter of a stone porch where the fierce gusts and little scuds of rain could no longer buffet her.

He hammered on the door, and the summons was greeted immediately by the deep, fierce baying of a dog within the house. For what seemed a long time no other sound was heard, but then a voice spoke sharply, the clamour subsided, and the door was opened an inch or two on a chain, letting out a feeble ray of light which revealed an unidentifiable figure beyond. Bernard spoke imperiously.

'Let us in, and tell Miss Crawthorne that her cousin, Mr Bernard Chard, and his wife have arrived!'

The first part of this command was not obeyed, but the figure turned its head and passed on the information to some other person in the hall. Katharine heard a woman say in a tone of blank astonishment:

'Bernard Chard? Good gracious, what in the world is *he* doing here?' A pause, and then: 'Well, do not keep them standing on the doorstep, Joseph! Open the door!'

This time the order was reluctantly obeyed, and the visitors stepped into the house. Katharine had a fleeting impression of a large, panelled hall, inadequately illuminated by a small lamp on a table at the foot of the stairs, of crowding shadows, and a general atmosphere of decay. A thin, plain woman in a shabby black dress was standing by the table, one hand resting on the neck of a huge dog which stared balefully at the intruders, and growled deep in its throat.

'Cousin Emma!' Bernard went forward, taking off his hat and holding out a hand in greeting, but Katharine hung back a little, nervously eyeing the dog. 'Can it be that you were not expecting us? Did you not receive my letter?'

Miss Crawthorne, shaking hands with him, murmured a bewildered denial, seeming to be quite at a loss. She looked small and frail beside the tall, broad-shouldered young man in the long, caped overcoat, and Katharine was conscious of a sudden pang of shame. Until that moment she had scarcely thought of Emma Crawthorne as a person. Bernard's back was towards her, but she did not need to see his face to know that he was completely in command of the situation and intended to remain so.

'I can't understand it,' he was saying easily. 'I wrote to tell that we were going down to Mallows, and would give ourselves the pleasure of visiting you on our way. The letter must have gone astray.'

'It does not matter. I am very glad to see you.' Emma was still bewildered, but she spoke civilly, her glance going past him to the girl whose cherry-red pelisse and bonnet glowed so richly against the shadowy background of the hall. 'I did not know, cousin, that you were married.'

'The event took place very recently, and since you are almost my only living kin I naturally wanted you to meet my wife.' He turned, putting out an imperative hand. 'Come, Kate!'

Katharine's eyes widened incredulously, and she stood frozen with shock and disbelief, seeing his face clearly for the first time since they had entered the house. Seeing, yet not understanding, the humorous curve of the lips, the mockery in the dark eyes, the small scar slanting above one lifted brow. Realizing, with a curious mixture of thankfulness, incredulity, and alarm, that the miracle she had longed for had in some mysterious fashion taken place, though in the shock of discovery it savoured rather of black magic. Bernard had vanished, and it was Brandon who stood beside her now.

11

In her overwrought state, the shock struck her with stunning force. Utterly incapable of speech or movement, she could only stand and stare, while the floor seemed to rock beneath her feet and her surroundings receded to a great distance. She heard Emma give an exclamation of concern, and then she was dimly conscious of Brandon picking her up and carrying her across the hall and into a room. Her eyes were closed, but after a moment she felt the welcome warmth of a fire. He sat her down in a chair and said calmly to Miss Crawthorne:

'Do not alarm yourself, cousin! I fancy the journey was a little too much for her, for she had been unwell and we have been on the road since early morning.'

'Poor child!' Emma's voice was full of sympathy. 'Wait, I will fetch my smelling-salts.'

Katharine heard her move quickly away. The faintness was passing, but she remained motionless and with closed eyes, delaying as long as possible the moment when she must face this new and incomprehensible situation. Brandon untied the strings of her bonnet and raised her head for a moment to remove the headgear, and then she felt his fingers at her throat, unfastening the tight collar of her pelisse, but she forced herself to remain still and apparently unaware of him. Only when Miss Crawthorne returned with the smelling-salts, and the pungent aroma of them made her gasp and catch her breath, did she open her eyes. She looked first into Emma's anxious face, and then past her to Brandon, who was standing just behind his cousin.

As her glance met his he moved to bend over her again, taking her hand in one of his while with the other he gently smoothed her hair. To Emma he must have seemed every inch the adoring husband, but Emma could not see the little devil of mockery that danced in his eyes.

'There, my love, you are better now!' His tone matched perfectly the pose he had chosen to adopt, and Katharine closed her eyes again, fighting against an almost overmastering desire to burst into tears. How and why Brandon had contrived to take his brother's place she could not guess, but after their last meeting this assumed tenderness was more than she could bear. She felt profoundly thankful when Emma said softly:

'Let her be, Bernard! She will feel more the thing when she has rested quietly for a little while. Did I understand you to say that you were on your way to Mallows?'

They moved away a little to the other side of the fireplace, and Katharine listened perplexedly to Brandon's easy, fluent explanations. Yes, they were going to Worcestershire. Katharine had been ailing, and, the doctor prescribing country air, his brother had suggested they should stay at Mallows until she was fully recovered. Her maid and his own manservant had been sent straight there with the bulk of the baggage, but he had decided to spend two days on the journey and pay a visit to Miss Crawthorne.

'For Brandon told me of your grandfather's death,' he concluded, 'and I felt it only proper to offer you any help which may lie within my power. We would have come before had Katharine's health permitted.'

'You are very kind, cousin!' Emma sounded genuinely grateful, and Katharine felt once again that uncomfortable prickle of shame. 'Things *are* difficult for a woman in my position, but I am fortunate in having the assistance of old Mr Spurling, who was Grandpapa's lawyer for many years. Your brother saw him, I understand, when he was here a few weeks ago. I felt it deeply that I was not well enough to receive Cousin Brandon myself, but it would have been quite ineligible, you know, for me to invite him to stay here! I do trust he does not think me excessively ungracious.'

'No such thing, I assure you! He understood perfectly. I hope, though, Cousin Emma, that you do not feel *our* presence to be an embarrassment to you?'

'No, indeed, how could I? The situation is entirely different. I only wish that I had received your letter, so that I might have made some provision. I am not at all in the way of entertaining, you know!'

'My dear Emma, pray do not put yourself about on our account. There is not the least need.'

'Well, it is very good of you to say so,' she replied dubiously, 'for I fear your welcome has left a great deal to be desired. Dear me, what am I thinking of? You will be needing some refreshment after travelling so far! Pray excuse me for a few minutes, and I will see to it.'

Katharine heard the door open and shut, and then Brandon's footsteps as he came back to the fire, but she kept her eyes closed even when he paused beside her. There was a moment or two of silence, during which she sensed that he was studying her, and then he said mockingly:

'You may open your eyes, Kate! We are alone, and there is for the moment no need for dissimulation.'

Indignation prompted her to obey him. She said sharply: 'I was not pretending! The shock of seeing you in Bernard's place all but robbed me of my senses. What possessed you to play such a trick upon me?'

'I merely wished to avoid a deal of fruitless argument. You were willing to come here posing as Bernard's wife, but you might have been less amenable once I had taken his place. You may recall that yesterday you expressed a fervent hope never to set eyes on me again.'

Recollection of all that had been said on that occasion brought the colour surging into her face. She turned her head away, saying in a constricted voice:

'What I may or may not do, sir, is surely no longer any concern of yours.'

'You think not?' Brandon's tone was sardonic. 'Believe me, Kate, the fact that you proposed to join with Bernard in imposing upon Emma Crawthorne is very much my concern.'

Her mind was clearer now, and she realized that there was only one point on the journey at which he could possibly have changed places with his brother, but the means used to effect the exchange mattered far less to her than the reason for it. If he had wished merely to expose the deception he need have done no more than come straight to the house.

'I suppose you took Bernard's place when the chaise was halted by that branch across the road?' she said after a moment, and he laughed.

'You are quite right! That spinney is an admirable spot for an ambush, and the branch lay very conveniently to hand at the roadside. It was the simplest thing imaginable to drag it across the track, and I knew that the post-boy would not be able to shift it unaided. Bernard would be bound to get down from the chaise to help him.'

She turned her head sharply to look at him. 'Then *you* could not have moved it by yourself, either!'

'Right again! I had the assistance of two very obliging friends who rode with me from London. They also assisted me in overcoming Bernard—easy enough with the darkness and the noise of the wind to cover our movements—and have undertaken to hold him prisoner in a convenient barn which we were fortunate enough to discover before night fell.'

He paused, studying her startled, incredulous face, and then chuckled softly. 'Don't look so astonished, Kate! A man acquires all manner of curious but useful accomplishments during years of military campaigning.'

'And curious but useful acquaintances also, it seems,' she retorted with more spirit than she felt. 'But you are not in Spain now, sir, and in this country it is against the law to kidnap people and hold them prisoner.' He bowed in acknowledgment of this, his eyes bright with amusement, and she turned angrily away again, saying over her shoulder: 'How did you know that we were coming here? I'll not believe that Bernard told you.'

'No, he did not. For reasons of my own I went to call upon him this morning, and his servant told me that he had gone out of town. After a certain amount of persuasion he also disclosed the fact that *he* had been sent out at an early hour to hire a chaise to carry his master to Stow-on-the-Wold. When he added that before entering the chaise Bernard instructed the post-boy to drive first to King Street, I had no doubt who was to go with him. The servant, you see, had already told me of a somewhat curious purchase which Bernard had ordered him to make this morning.' With an unexpected movement he grasped Katharine's left wrist in one hand, while with the other he stripped off her glove. The wedding ring which Bernard had given her to wear gleamed in the candlelight. 'You think of everything, don't you?' Brandon added contemptuously. 'It would not surprise me to learn that you had provided yourself with forged marriage-lines also.'

She snatched her hand away and thrust it out of

sight behind her, her cheeks scarlet with humiliation. He laughed shortly but did not pursue the subject.

'It seemed odd to me,' he remarked musingly, 'that you should come to this house, of all places. I was sure that Bernard could not be going into hiding, or he would have covered his tracks more carefully, but I knew that he must have some purpose, probably a dishonest one. So my friends and I followed, and because we came on horseback were able to travel faster than you did. During the journey I conceived the idea of taking Bernard's place, since for all I knew he might have written to Emma to announce your coming.'

She looked curiously at him. 'Were you not afraid that I would cry out the truth as soon as I saw your face?'

He shrugged. 'I gambled on the belief that you would be too much taken aback to say anything until you had had time to consider the situation. As you see, I was right!'

'I might do so yet.'

He shook his head. 'I don't think you will, Kate! If you tell Emma that I am not Bernard I shall be obliged to tell her that *you* are not Bernard's wife. We cannot betray each other without betraying ourselves.' He watched dismayed, reluctant acceptance of his words creep into her eyes, and the mockery in his own face deepened. 'Precisely, my dear Mrs Chard! We are committed to the masquerade for as long as we remain in this house.'

Miss Crawthorne coming back into the room at that moment, Katharine was spared the necessity of making any reply to this. Emma regarded her closely, and remarked with satisfaction that she was glad to see her looking more the thing, and with some colour in her cheeks. Katharine, rousing herself to play the part which had been thrust upon her, was obliged to thank her, and to beg pardon for any alarm she might have caused.

Emma then proceeded to set the table for a meal, explaining that she was obliged to perform such tasks herself since old Joseph and Bertha, his wife, were the only servants she had, unless one counted the aged Timothy, who lived alone in the lodge and did what he could to keep the gardens from becoming a complete wilderness.

'And I cannot tell you, cousin, how thankful I shall be to be rid of this tumbledown barn of a house,' she told Brandon earnestly. 'Why anyone should wish to buy it I cannot imagine, but Mr Spurling tells me that he has received a tolerable offer for it; tolerable enough, at all events, to provide me with a cottage in the village. Joseph and Bertha will come with me, and I shall have my dear dog for company. It seems almost too good to be true.'

The dear dog, which had accompanied its mistress into the room, ambled forward and sat down in front of the fire. Its head reached the level of Katharine's shoulder, and it yawned cavernously, disclosing powerful, admirably equipped jaws, so that she shrank back a little in her chair. It seemed incredible that the frail Miss Crawthorne could regard this terrifying beast as a pet. Brandon, who had been watching, said with some amusement:

'I fear, cousin, that my wife does not share your

THE RELUCTANT ADVENTURESS 173

enthusiasm for the dog. In fact, she is frightened half to death by it.'

'Oh, my dear Mrs Chard, there is not the least need,' Emma assured her patronizingly. 'He is exceedingly intelligent, you know, and will not harm you now that he has seen me make you welcome. Of course, if anyone broke into the house, or offered me any violence, it would be a very different matter.'

Katharine, dubiously eyeing the enormous animal, found herself unable to derive much comfort from these words, and was glad when the dog subsided on to the floor and went to sleep. After a little while an old woman came into the room with a loaded tray, and Miss Crawthorne invited her guests to table, apologizing as she did so that she had no better fare to offer.

It was indeed a somewhat meagre repast, but Katharine, who felt that every mouthful she swallowed must choke her, could have wished it even smaller. She said very little during the meal, but tried to occupy her thoughts by taking surreptitious stock of her surroundings and of her hostess. The room in which they sat was of moderate size, and appeared to serve both as parlour and dining-room. The furniture was heavy and old-fashioned, and the curtains and cushions threadbare; there were darns in the white damask tablecloth, and the dishes and cutlery were of the plainest kind.

Miss Crawthorne's appearance matched that of her surroundings. Her black dress was rusty, and looked as though it had been inexpertly made over from one belonging to a much plumper lady, while her hands, though elegantly long and narrow, were roughened by housework. Looking at her, Katharine could not deny that Bernard's spiteful description was justified. Emma Crawthorne was exceedingly plain, and could never, even in the full flush of girlhood, have been otherwise. Her face was thin, with a long nose and a prim, rather tight-lipped mouth; her complexion sallow; and her lank hair, unbecomingly dressed beneath a plain cap, a nondescript shade of brown. In figure she was angular, with slightly stooping shoulders, and her whole air was one of harassed timidity, as though she had been used to constant bullying. She was in her early thirties, but looked at least ten years older.

Brandon appeared to be completely at ease, and if he experienced any difficulty in assuming his brother's identity, gave no sign of it. His task was made easier by the fact that Miss Crawthorne had seen neither twin for years, but it would not have been remarkable, Katharine thought, if he had hesitated a little. He did not, even when his hostess spoke, as she did more than once, of Captain Chard.

'Do you find your brother much altered, Bernard?' she asked at one point, adding to Katharine: 'I dare say you will not be surprised to know, ma'am, that as children it was almost impossible to tell them apart.'

'Oh, we are still taken for each other occasionally,' Brandon replied easily as Katharine murmured some polite response. 'Even Kate has been known to experience a trifling difficulty in that respect.'

Miss Crawthorne permitted herself a prim smile at what she took to be a jest, but went on to ask whether the Captain had come back to England for good.

'Perhaps,' she suggested, 'he will follow your example, cousin, and find himself a wife. Mallows has already been left too long without a mistress, and by now he must surely have had a surfeit of travel and adventure.'

'I doubt whether he will ever weary of either, cousin,' Brandon said lightly. 'As for marriage—well, there was one lady he asked to be his wife, but for reasons best known to herself, she would have none of him. Is that not so, Kate?'

Goaded by the undercurrent of mockery in his words, she ventured to raise her head and look at him across the table, to encounter a glance she could not understand. Amusement was there, certainly, as it had been ever since they faced each other in the hall, but now she could see perplexity as well, the hint of an unspoken question. For a moment it was as though the bitter quarrel of the previous day had never happened, and then Emma spoke again, he turned to answer her, and Katharine was left to wonder whether she had imagined that brief softening of his glance.

By the time the meal was over the hands of the clock on the mantelpiece pointed to twenty minutes to ten, and Miss Crawthorne announced that she would take Katharine up to her bedchamber.

'No doubt you sit up later than this in London,' she added, 'but Grandpapa always insisted upon the whole household being in bed before ten o'clock, and such habits die hard. Besides, after so long a journey I expect you will both be glad to retire.'

Katharine sought frantically for some excuse to delay, but could think of none which would not offend Miss Crawthorne, who had got up from her chair and was waiting for her guest to do likewise. With the utmost reluctance Katharine did so, and followed her across the room. Brandon, who had also risen courteously to his feet, went to open the door for them; she could not bring herself to look at him, but felt certain that he had read her thoughts and was laughing at her.

12

In the hall Miss Crawthorne lit a candle from the lamp burning there and took Katharine up the handsome, seventeenth-century staircase to the first floor. Leading the way along an echoing corridor where bare, rectangular patches on the panelled walls showed where pictures had once hung, she said over her shoulder:

'I told Bertha to prepare Grandpapa's room for you. I do hope you will not object to sleeping there, but to be frank with you, my dear ma'am—and since you are one of the family I am sure there can be no need to be otherwise—it is the only bedroom in the house, apart from my own and the servants', which is at all habitable. To be sure, it is not a very cheerful apartment, but I am persuaded you have too much common sense to be alarmed by that.'

She paused, and opened a door on to what appeared to be a small antechamber, where a truckle-bed stood against one wall. Crossing to another door on the far side of the room, she went on:

'This is the dressing-room, of course, but after Grandpapa became bedridden I was obliged to sleep here. He very often needed attention during the night, and he would have no one else to nurse him.'

Opening the other door, she passed into the inner room, and Katharine, reluctantly following, found herself in the gloomiest apartment she had ever seen. A small fire burned on the cavernous hearth, its feeble light flickering over walls panelled with age-blackened oak from floor to moulded ceiling. An immense four-poster dominated the room. It was hung with moth-eaten plum-coloured velvet, and curtains of the same sombre hue, stirred weirdly by the draught, masked two tall windows. The wind howled round the house and moaned in the wide chimney; heavy, carved furniture cast menacing shadows; and in one corner a large tall-case clock, its hands motionless at twelve o'clock, brooded like some baleful sentinel. Even Miss Crawthorne seemed to be aware of the room's eerie atmosphere, for she began to move fussily about, lighting more candles, stirring the fire, and smoothing the heavily embroidered velvet quilt which covered the bed.

'I do trust, Mrs Chard, that you will be comfortable,' she said dubiously. 'This is a very old house, so you must not be alarmed if you hear any curious sounds, for one frequently finds such, you know, in ancient buildings. That clock does not go, I fear. It has been quite useless for years, but Grandpapa would not part with it.' She sighed. 'Old folk have such odd fancies! He even insisted upon it being brought up here from his study after he became confined to his bed, and *such* a time we had shifting it! Do not be disturbed if you hear the dog moving about. I always allow him to roam loose in the house during the night.' She paused, studying the younger woman with some concern. 'Do you feel quite well, my dear? You are most dreadfully pale. Perhaps, since your maid is not here, I ought to help you to bed.'

'No!' Katharine spoke with an effort, forcing her lips into some semblance of a smile. 'No, thank you, it is not at all necessary. I am just a little tired, that is all.'

'Well, to be sure, that is no wonder, after travelling all the way from London in one day. I cannot imagine why Bernard was so unthinking!' Emma drifted towards the door as she spoke. 'I fear he is not greatly like his brother, except in looks. Brandon Chard is one of the kindest people I have ever met.'

She went out, and Katharine, after one hunted glance about her, sank into the shabby, high-backed armchair beside the fire and covered her face with her hands. A few days earlier she would have agreed unhesitatingly with Miss Crawthorne's estimate of Brandon's character, but in her present situation so comforting a certainty was denied her. If he had had any doubt at all of the truth of the accusations he had hurled at her the previous day, her flight with Bernard must surely have dispelled it. He believed her to be dishonest as well as wanton, and she could see no hope of convincing him that she was neither.

At last the sound of his footsteps in the outer room brought her to her feet in panic, staring wildly towards the door. It opened, and Brandon paused on the threshold, looking about him with the liveliest astonishment.

'Good God!' he remarked. 'What a devilish room! One can almost hear the family ghost rattling its chains!' Then his gaze passed from his forbidding surroundings to Katharine's shrinking figure, poised as though for flight, and laughter leapt into his eyes again. He closed the door and strolled towards her, saying in a tone of mingled exasperation and amusement: 'Oh, stop looking so terror-stricken, Kate! Sit down, and tell me *why* you and Bernard decided to come here.'

A little reassured by his manner, she reluctantly obeyed the first part of his command, but found it less easy to comply with the second. Brandon propped his shoulders against the side of the great stone fireplace and regarded her inquiringly.

'Well?' he said with a hint of impatience, when a few moments had crept past in silence. 'I want the truth, Kate, and I want it now! Bernard has been toying with the notion of visiting this house ever since he heard that Jasper Crawthorne was dead. Why? He never puts himself to any trouble unless he expects to gain something from it.'

'He believes that old Mr Crawthorne owned jewels worth a fortune, and that they are hidden here,' she replied in a low voice. 'Miss Crawthorne's brother told him so. He wanted to find them before the house was sold.'

Stated thus baldly, the facts sounded preposterous even to Katharine herself, and she was not surprised

THE RELUCTANT ADVENTURESS   181

to see a look of scepticism in Brandon's face. Stammering a little, she recounted the whole story as Bernard had told it to her, and did not know whether to be glad or sorry when she saw that he was beginning to take her seriously.

'I suppose it *is* possible,' he said slowly when she paused. 'We used to come here on visits as children, when Emma's parents were alive, and there was certainly no lack of money then. I always imagined, if I thought of it at all, that the old man had lost his fortune through unlucky speculation or something of that sort.'

'But surely,' she suggested timidly, 'if Mr Crawthorne did possess so valuable a treasure he would have told Miss Emma of it before he died. Or at least left a will disclosing the existence of the jewels. He would not deliberately leave her in poverty.'

Brandon shook his head. 'I doubt if towards the end he was capable of such reasoned thought, and even when he was in his right mind Emma's welfare was the last thing that concerned him. No, if Freddy's story was true, and not some drunken fancy, the jewels are still hidden in this house. Probably in this room!'

'Here?' Katharine cast a startled glance about her. 'But would they not have been discovered by now?'

'Why should they be? You may depend that the old man would have a cunning hiding-place for them. There may be a sliding panel, or a cavity under the floor—the house is very old! Or there could be a secret compartment somewhere in the furniture. This was old Jasper's room, and he would have wished to keep his treasure close to him.'

'Then let us look for it!' Katharine jumped up, feigning an eagerness she did not really feel, but Brandon stretched out his hand and grasped her by the wrist, holding her prisoner beside him. Lifting her frightened gaze to his face, she saw that he was once more regarding her with a puzzled look in his eyes.

'That can wait!' he said abruptly. 'Kate, why did you tell Tillingham that you were Bernard's mistress?'

'Bernard said that, not I!' She was trembling, but her gaze met his steadily. 'It is not true, I swear it!'

'No?' His voice was level, betraying neither scepticism or belief. 'That Bernard is capable of such a lie I know, and had it come only from him I would not have credited it for an instant. But you had told Tillingham it was true. That I could not understand.'

'I could have explained it, had you asked me,' she whispered. 'Oh, why did you not?'

'I intended to,' he replied. 'When you gave me those letters yesterday I realized that there was something which made no sense. I came to the house last night, but was refused admittance. This morning I went to Bernard's lodging, meaning to choke the truth out of him if I could come at it in no other way, but he had already gone. So I am asking you now, Kate! Why did you do it?'

'Because I did not know what Bernard had said. Edward was plaguing me to elope with him, and I feared that my uncle would force me to go with him. Bernard offered to tell Edward that it had all been a plot, and that I had deliberately set out to captivate him. That was what I thought I was confessing to. I knew nothing of the rest.'

He continued to hold her, his dark eyes searching her face as though he wished to believe her yet found it difficult to do so. At length he said in a hard voice:

'I would find that easier to credit if we were still in London. If Bernard betrayed your trust in that fashion, why did you consent to come here posing as his wife? You cannot be so innocent that you did not know what that would mean.'

She turned her head away, the colour rushing into her face. 'Yes, but I was desperate! You do not know . . .'

'I do not know what punishment your uncle inflicted upon you for returning those letters? No, I do not, but you are going to tell me. Yes, Kate, you are! What brought you to such a pitch of despair that you were prepared to turn to Bernard to escape it?'

After a little, in a low, shamed voice, she told him. She could not bring herself to look at him as she spoke, and so did not see the expression in his face, but his grip on her wrist tightened suddenly so that she gave a little gasp of pain. He released her immediately and she dropped into the chair again, her face still averted.

'That horrible old man!' she whispered with an uncontrollable shudder. 'I could not endure that! I could not! So I agreed to go with Bernard. There was no one else I could turn to.'

'No,' he agreed in an odd voice, 'there was no one else. An ingenious fellow, your uncle, and rarely at a stand!' He was silent for a moment, and then gently touched her wrist, where his fingers had left a red mark. 'I hurt you, Kate! I am sorry.'

She made a little gesture of denial, but still did not look at him. The truth had been told and he seemed to believe it, but the knowledge brought none of the relief she had expected. She felt numbed, incapable of further emotion, neither knowing nor greatly caring what was to follow. Brandon stood watching her for a little while, a good deal of understanding in his eyes, and then he turned thoughtfully to survey the room. He moved closer to the wall beside the fireplace and began to tap experimentally on each panel in turn.

Katherine looked up quickly at his first movement, and after watching him for a little while, got up and went slowly towards him. He glanced round at her and smiled.

'Best to lose no time if we are to find those jewels,' he said lightly. 'It's not likely that we can prolong our visit indefinitely.'

She nodded, and said in a voice which was only a little unsteady: 'Suppose someone hears?'

He shook his head. 'Unlikely, I imagine, for the walls must be very thick. The only danger is that the dog may be aroused, but he, I trust, is in some other part of the house.'

She made no reply, but went to the opposite wall and began to test the panels there, tapping on them as she had seen Brandon do. For more than two hours they searched, proving the walls and floor, examining the carving of the fireplace, and investigating the ornate old-fashioned furniture, but without the smallest success. At last Katharine sank down on the foot of the bed and leaned her head wearily against one of the massive posts. The fire had gone out, and she was shivering in her thin muslin dress.

'It is no use,' she said in a discouraged voice. 'If the jewels do exist they must be hidden somewhere else in the house. We have looked everywhere in here.'

'It certainly seems so,' he agreed, 'and yet I cannot imagine old Jasper not keeping them in his own room.' He had paused beside the big clock, and now turned to study it thoughtfully. 'We did not try the panels behind this. The other pieces of furniture are obviously too heavy to move, but this may be a different matter.'

He laid hold of the clock as he spoke and tried to move it out from its corner. It shifted a little, but not until he had exerted all his strength, and after a moment he abandoned the attempt.

'The old man could never have moved it without assistance, that's certain,' he said, 'so there is little point in searching behind it.' He brushed some dust from his coat, eyeing the ponderous timepiece with some irritation. 'How like Emma to give houseroom to a damned great clock that doesn't even work.'

'She told me it has not gone for years!' Katharine's voice was hoarse with fatigue. 'But her grandfather was fond of it, and insisted upon it being brought up here when he became bedridden—' She broke off, staring at Brandon with an arrested expression as the same thought occurred to both of them.

'Did he, by Jupiter?' he said softly, 'I wonder why?'

He turned to examine the clock more closely, and Katharine got up and went to join him. They had already looked inside the massive case, but now they began to go over it inch by inch, and at last Brandon, kneeling on the floor in front of it, uttered an exclamation and said in a tone of suppressed excitement:

'Kate, pass me that candle! I believe we have hit upon something!'

Breathlessly she obeyed him, her weariness forgotten in a rising tide of excitement. He held the candle inside the clock-case, shading the flame with his hand and peering downwards, then set it down and plunged both arms inside. There was a faint click, and his hands emerged holding the solid-looking piece of wood which had formed the floor of the case. He set this down also and then reached in again, and this time lifted out a sturdy wooden casket, hinged and banded with brass.

Its lid was secured by a padlock, but without hesitation he fetched a poker from the fireplace and with this succeeded in forcing the hasp. He lifted the lid, and a piece of soft leather beneath it, and a glint and glimmer from within told that the search was at an end. Brandon carried the box to the bed and tipped its contents out on the coverlet, and then they both stood very still, staring, fascinated and almost disbelieving, at the fantastic heap glittering in the light of the guttering candles against the dark, worn velvet. Diamonds for the most part, but with here and there the richer colour of rubies and emeralds. The whole fortune of a wealthy family, compressed at the whim of a crazed old man into one small box.

'So Freddy was right, and Bernard spoke the truth for once in his life,' Brandon said softly at last. 'Well, Kate, there it is! A fortune which you could hold in your hands!'

'It is . . . incredible!' she murmured, and put out one tentative finger to touch the flashing stones as though she half expected them to vanish at a touch. 'I never dreamed that finding them would be so easy.' Then a thought occurred to her and she looked sharply up at him. 'What are you going to do now?'

He did not reply at once, but then said, without lifting his gaze from the jewels: 'What did Bernard intend?'

'To keep them, of course,' she replied scornfully. 'To steal them from his cousin and go abroad. He said that she would not know what to do with half such a sum, but would be far happier living in a country village and busying herself with good works.'

Brandon chuckled. 'He may be right! In fact, I am sure he is! Poor Emma would be scared half out of her wits by the responsibility of such a fortune.'

'I don't understand,' she faltered. 'You do mean to give them to her, do you not?'

'Give them to her?' He withdrew his gaze at last from the jewels and turned to face her, setting his hands on her shoulders. 'My lovely Kate, what manner of fool do you think I am? There is a fortune there for the taking. We have only to hide that box in your portmanteau, and in the morning bid a civil farewell to Emma and go on our way. What could be simpler?'

She stared at him, shocked and incredulous, stabbed by a disillusionment so sharp that it was like a physical pain. 'You would not steal them, when she is so poor?'

'This house is as good as sold, and will bring her enough for a cottage in the village. That is all she wants. You heard her say so! A cottage, and her two old servants, and her dog.' He laughed down into Katharine's white face. 'Let her have them! *We'll* take the jewels, and all the pleasures they can buy for us. But you shall wear the best of them, Kate! Beauty like yours deserves such gems.'

She continued to stare at him as though reluctant to believe the evidence of her senses. 'You are very sure that I will go with you!'

'What alternative have you? A return to London, to Carforth, or to some other protector of the same kind? No, you will do better to marry me. For I *will* marry you, Kate, which is more than my brother would have done.'

He let her go, and turned away to sweep the jewels back into their box, while Katharine stood frozen with shock and pain. He tucked the box under his arm, and then dragged the heavy quilt from the bed and flung it carelessly across his shoulder. He glanced at her, and she saw the mockery glinting again in his eyes.

'I'll take the bed in the dressing-room,' he said, and sauntered across to the door, the worn velvet trailing jauntily behind him. There he turned and made her an ironic bow. 'Good night, my dear!

You may barricade this door behind me if you choose, but I give you my word it is not in the least necessary.'

13

When Katharine finally climbed into the enormous bed she had little expectation of sleeping, but so tired was she that not all the doubts and perplexities which beset her mind had the power to keep her awake. She sank almost at once into a deep slumber, from which she was roused only by daylight falling suddenly across her face. She uttered a drowsy murmur of protest and flung one arm across her eyes, and Brandon's voice said in a tone of some amusement:

'Come, Kate, wake up! Upon my word, you sleep like the dead!'

In the first moment of waking she had scarcely been aware of her surroundings, but the sound of his voice jerked her fully awake and she started up on her elbow. Before retiring she had drawn the heavy curtains about the bed, but now one of them had been pulled aside and Brandon, still holding it, was looking down at her. The window-hangings had also been flung back, and the room was full of sunlight so strong and golden that she knew the morning must be well advanced. Brandon was fully and immaculately dressed, and had the appearance of one who had been up and about for a considerable time. Confused and embarrased, she stared back at him, and was even more disconcerted by his next remark, delivered in the same humorous tone.

'But you wake very prettily! That is an accomplishment few women possess.'

Colour surged into her face. She sat, clutching the bedclothes about her, and said with as much dignity as she could command: 'Have I slept very late? What time is it?'

'Past ten o'clock, and time you got up if we are to be on our way by noon. I sent the chaise back to the village last night and told the post-boy to wait there for my orders, so I am now going to walk down to the inn to fetch him. You will have to take charge of this meanwhile.'

He set the casket containing the jewels down on the bed, and Katharine looked at it with a sinking heart. Brandon went on.

'I could, of course, send Joseph or the gardener for the chaise, but the fact is that I engaged to meet one of my obliging friends at eleven o'clock in the spinney where we stopped the chaise last night. Something must be arranged about Bernard. We cannot keep him prisoner indefinitely.' He saw the look of horror in her eyes, and laughed. 'Put your mind at ease! I do not propose to murder him. No one is likely to pay heed to any tale he may tell, and in any event you and I will be out of England before he has a chance to tell it. I've no doubt that my friends will escort him back to London once I have settled matters with them.'

'I suppose you mean when you have paid them off,' she retorted, and he laughed again.

'Perhaps I do! I believe that from this point on we shall need no company but our own. Take care of that box, Kate! By the time you have dressed and eaten your breakfast the chaise should be here.'

He was turning away. Katharine, her gaze still fixed miserably on the box, said urgently: 'Brandon!'

'Yes?' He turned, a half smile on his lips, the quizzical eyebrow raised. She lifted her eyes to meet his, and could find no words to express her conflicting emotions. She shook her head.

'It does not matter. I will do as you say.'

For a second or two longer he continued to regard her with an expression she could not read, and then he moved away and the drawn bed-curtains hid him from her. She heard the door close behind him, and after a moment bent forward and drew the casket towards her. Leaning back against the pillows, she set it on her lap and lifted the lid, and the fabulous glitter of the jewels blazed up at her, more dazzling now than it had been by candlelight.

For several minutes she sat staring at them, fighting a bitter battle within herself, and then, her decision taken, shut the lid with a snap and thrust the casket aside. She could not even guess how Brandon would react to betrayal, but she knew that she could never fall in with his plan to rob Emma Crawthorne of her inheritance.

She jumped out of bed and began hastily to

dress. In the morning sunshine the room which had seemed so sinister the night before was now merely pathetically shabby, and the windows, framed by the ivy which covered the house like a green mantle, showed a tangle of neglected garden, and beyond that a splendid vista of hill and valley. The countryside was no longer harsh and hostile, but smiling in all the pride of early summer, and the beauty of it pierced her with sudden pain. There was a coldness about her heart, and dread of the future lay like a leaden weight on her spirits.

She had finished dressing and was putting the last of her belongings into the portmanteau when a soft tap on the door was followed by the entry into the room of Miss Crawthorne, bearing a tray. She looked suprised to see her guest already up, and set the tray down, saying in her anxious way:

'My dear Mrs Chard, I did not know you had already risen, or I would have sent Bertha up with a can of hot water. Bernard would not have us disturb you earlier, but he told me before he went out that you were awake, and so I thought I would bring a breakfast tray up to you.'

'It is very good of you, ma'am, but indeed, I did not wish to put you to any trouble,' Katharine replied. 'Our visit has inconvenienced you more than enough as it is.'

'No, no, I assure you! You must not be thinking any such thing. I am exceedingly happy to have seen Bernard again, and to have made *your* acquaintance. You are my only living relatives, you know.' She turned back to the tray and began to pour coffee into a cup, adding rather wistfully: 'And Brandon, of couse! I wish so much that I had been able to receive him when he called, for it is seven years since last we met. He was on furlough from Spain, you know. Such a dashing young officer, so gay . . . and so very kind!'

Katharine, accepting the coffee with a murmur of thanks, did not know what reply to make to this. She had noticed the previous evening how Miss Crawthorne seized every opportunity to bring Brandon's name into the conversation, and had an uneasy suspicion that she cherished warmer feelings towards him than were warranted by their distant kinship and comparatively slight acquaintance. Katharine could sympathize with her to the full, but it made the present situation even more awkward, and she hoped fervently that she would be able to keep the true identity of her supposed husband secret from their hostess.

Miss Crawthorne, meanwhile, had been studying the younger woman in a fascinated way. She had thought from the moment of setting eyes on her that Bernard's wife was the most beautiful creature she had ever seen, and now that the pinched look of weariness she had worn the previous evening had been smoothed away, she felt quite dazzled by her. Her face and figure, the elegance of that deceptively simple white dress with its discreet trimming of lace and cherry-coloured ribbon, made her seem to Emma like the inhabitant of another world. She did not begrudge Katharine her good looks, but she was not yet so old herself that she did not feel a tiny pang of envy.

Katharine drank the coffee, set down the cup, and, paying no heed to Emma's stream of diffident, inconsequential talk, walked across to the bed where the casket still lay, half hidden by the tumbled bedclothes. Picking it up, she lifted the lid and turned, holding the box out towards her companion.

'These belong to you, Miss Crawthorne,' she said simply. 'They were your grandfather's.'

The sunlight fell full and strong upon the open box, so that its contents blazed and flashed with rainbow-coloured fire. Emma put up one hand as though to shade her eyes, while with the other she groped for and found a chair. She dropped into it, uttering faintly:

'What did you say?'

'These jewels belong to you,' Katharine repeated. She set the casket down on the other woman's lap, and dropped to her knees beside the chair. 'That is where all your grandfather's money went, first because he feared the French invasion, and later because he suffered from the delusion that everyone wanted to rob him. Your brother knew of it, and he told Bernard. That is why we came here.'

'Grandpapa had these jewels, although he pretended we were so poor?' Emma said dazedly. 'Heaven preserve us! They must be worth a fortune!' She touched the glittering gems with one work-roughened hand as though unable to believe in the reality of them. 'But I do not understand! How did you come by them? Why did I never know about them?'

Quietly Katharine explained, describing the search they had made, and how Emma's own words had led them eventually to the hiding-place. Miss Crawthorne listened incredulously, and at the end said in a wondering tone:

'I cannot quite believe it! For the first time in my life I shall be able to do exactly as I please—and I owe it all to you and Bernard. How shall I ever be able to repay you?'

Katharine rose to her feet and stood looking down at her, her hands twisted tightly together, a painful flush darkening her cheeks. 'You must not speak of repayment,' she said in a low voice. 'It shames me to confess it, but our first intention was to keep the jewels for ourselves. Bernard still has that intention. He must not know that I have given them to you.'

For several moments Miss Crawthorne continued to stare at her in a puzzled fashion, then she looked again at the open box on her lap. She said diffidently: 'I have not the least idea of the value of these jewels, but I am sure it must be very great. More than enough for all of us.'

'No!' Katharine spoke sharply. 'You must not suggest such a thing. You must not speak of it to him at all.'

'But, child, I should be quite happy to share them with you. My wants are modest, and if Bernard is in such desperate need that he was prepared to steal——'

'He *wants* the jewels,' Katharine broke in bitterly, 'but between wanting and needing there is a world of difference. Oh, dear ma'am, do you not understand? *Sharing* them would not be enough!'

'My head is in such a whirl that I do not understand anything,' Emma said plaintively, 'least of all why you should give me the jewels if your husband is determined to keep them.'

'I am not a thief, Miss Crawthorne,' Katharine

replied with a sigh, 'nor do I wish to see *him* become one. But those jewels offer a great temptation, and I fear that no persuasions of yours *or* mine could prevail against them. So I beg of you, say nothing at all to him when he returns.'

'But he will know that you no longer have them.'

Katharine shook her head. 'No, I think not—at least not until it is too late for us to return for them. I will take the empty box, and it will never occur to him that the jewels are not still inside it.'

'But will he not be excessively angry when he finds out what you have done?'

'Yes, but I am not afraid of that,' Katharine replied untruthfully. She did not know what would happen when Brandon learned how he had been tricked, and she did not even want to think about it. 'And you must not disturb yourself on my account.'

She broke off, for the outer door of the dressing-room had opened. Emma sat as though paralysed, the casket still open on her lap, but Katharine snatched it up and darted across to the bed, where she thrust it out of sight again beneath the covers. She swung around as a knock fell upon the bedroom door, and said in a tolerably steady voice: 'Come in.'

The door opened to admit the old manservant. He cast an apologetic glance at Katharine, but addressed himself instead to her companion.

'Oh, there you be, Miss Emma! Bertha said like as not I'd find you with the young lady. Dunno what the place be coming to, what with all these comings and goings. The master wouldn't have liked it above half.'

These words conveyed nothing to Katharine, but

Emma, accustomed to her henchman's way of expressing himself, seemed to find no difficulty in interpreting them. Looking at him in the liveliest astonishment, she asked:

'Do you mean, Joseph, that I have yet another visitor?'

'Aye, that you have! 'Tis the other one this time, though they be that like a man's hard put to it to tell one from t'other.' He saw that the two ladies were still staring at him, Katharine blankly, Miss Crawthorne with an expression in which astonishment was now giving way to delight, and added belatedly: ''Tis Mr Brandon. Captain Chard, I *should* say!'

Katharine, still standing by the bed, was thankful for the support of its massive post, for the announcement had set her trembling violently. What could have happened, what madness taken possession of Brandon to make him return to the house in his own name within an hour of leaving it as Bernard? It had been easy enough to pass himself off as his twin when Emma had seen neither of them for years, but it was absurd to suppose that she could be deceived in this fashion.

Joseph's news had naturally not dealt Miss Crawthorne the same stunning blow it had inflicted on Katharine. She waved the servant away, saying rather breathlessly:

'Thank you, Joseph. Pray tell the Captain I will join him directly.' She waited until the old man had gone, and then turned to Katharine, saying eagerly: 'My dear Mrs Chard, what could be more fortunate? Cousin Brandon will know exactly what should be done.'

'You must not tell him!' Katharine's voice was

sharp with dismay. 'Miss Crawthorne, I beg of you, say nothing about the jewels.'

'Of course we must tell him,' Emma replied indulgently, getting up from the chair. 'I have the greatest faith imaginable in Brandon's judgment and common sense, and though I dare say you would prefer no one else to know what Bernard meant to do, there can be no harm in telling his brother. No doubt he will give Bernard a great scold, but we can depend upon him to set this sad tangle to rights.'

She hurried out of the room without paying any further heed to Katharine's protests, and Katharine sank down on the edge of the bed and stared helplessly after her. She was inexperienced herself, but Miss Crawthorne's naive innocence made her feel immeasurably wise in the ways of the world. Emma seemed to regard the attempt to steal the jewels as a boyish prank; she had apparently no idea of their real value, or of the lengths to which unscrupulous persons would go to lay hands on such a prize.

It occurred to Katharine that it might be prudent to know what Emma and Brandon were saying to each other, and she was halfway across the dressing-room before another thought halted her. The jewels! They could not be left lying upon the bed, for it was only to be expected that Brandon would lose no time in taking possession of them again as soon as he discovered what she had done. She ran back to the bedroom and dragged the casket from its hiding-place, determined somehow to thwart his intention. Previously it had been simply a matter of conscience, but now the gems had become a danger which not even their great value could outweigh, for it was not to be supposed that Emma would keep her knowledge to herself. She would tell the lawyer, and he would inform the authorities. At best, Brandon would become a hunted criminal, unable ever to return to England once he had left it. At worst, he would be apprehended, flung into prison, perhaps even hanged. A whole galaxy of hideous possibilities flashed through Katharine's mind as she stood clutching the box to her breast and looking frantically about her for some place in which to hide it.

The clock? No, for Brandon knew the trick of that now, just as he knew every other possible hiding place in the room. The exhaustive search the night before had made certain of that. Yet it would be foolhardy to venture farther afield, for she was totally unfamiliar with the house and the time at her disposal was likely to be short.

At last a possibility occurred to her, and she ran to the nearest window. The casement was stiff from long disuse, so that she was obliged to put down the box and use both hands before she could force it open, but after a struggle she succeeded. The wind ruffled her hair as she leaned out, and she saw that, as she had hoped, the ivy cloaking the house was old and very thick. After a quick glance about to assure herself that the overgrown garden was deserted, she stretched out as far as she dared, parted the leaves, and wedged the box securely between two gnarled and twisted stems. When she withdrew her hands the glossy leaves sprang back into place, effectively screening the box from any but the most searching regard.

She tugged the window shut again, straightened

the curtain, and stood back to study the result. As far as she could see, there was nothing to indicate that they had ever been disturbed. With great deliberation she wiped the dust from her fingers, smoothed her hair, and then, assuming an air of self-possession to disguise the apprehension she felt, went slowly down to the parlour.

When she reached the door she could hear Miss Crawthorne's voice speaking breathlessly within, though she could not distinguish the words. She drew a deep breath, pushed open the door, and stepped into the room, and Emma stopped talking abruptly. She was sitting in a chair beside the fire with her great dog stretched out at her feet, while her visitor stood looking down at her, his back to the door.

Katharine stopped short, staring in astonishment, dismay, and growing alarm. Brandon, when last she saw him, had been wearing riding-dress—an olive-green coat, buckskins, and top-boots. This man's coat was blue, and considerably creased; he wore dove-coloured pantaloons, and Hessian boots spattered with mud, and Katharine had no difficulty at all in recognizing this attire.

'You!' she said in a low, frightened voice. 'How —how do you come to be here?'

Bernard turned slowly to face her. He was unshaven, and his neckcloth and shirt-collar were limp and grubby, and he had a jaunty air and looked remarkably pleased with himself.

'Didn't expect to see me again, did you, Katharine?' he said in a satisfied tone. 'It was a neat trick you played on me, my dear, but you and that brother of mine are not quite as clever as you suppose.'

14

Slowly Katharine closed the door and leaned against it, trying to control her hurrying thoughts. So Bernard had escaped from his captors, and obviously Miss Crawthorne had no suspicion of his real identity. Katharine would have liked to think that Emma had as yet said nothing about the jewels, but Bernard's air of barely concealed triumph told her that the hope was vain.

'Only fancy, my dear,' Emma said earnestly, 'poor Brandon was set upon by robbers last night, only a short distance from here. It is a miracle that his life was spared, and yet he does not seem to regard it in the least.'

Her tone, and the anxious, admiring glance at Bernard which accompanied it, showed only too clearly that she had accepted his story without question. Katharine, looking him squarely in the eye, said ironically:

'You forget, ma'am, that he is a soldier. I am sure he endured far more perilous adventures during his service in Spain. What I cannot understand is how he happened to be so close behind us.'

She hoped to throw Bernard into some disorder by this challenge, but the shot went wide. He grinned impudently at her.

'My dear girl, can't you guess? I thought it was a dashed queer start when I heard that you meant to come here, for, without wishing to offend Cousin Emma, it seemed to me the last place in the world you would want to visit. So I decided to ride after you and find out what game you were playing, and, from what Emma has just told me, it's a deuced good thing I did.'

Katharine looked at Miss Crawthorne. 'What *did* you tell him, ma'am?' she asked quietly.

'Why, everything, to be sure, for you know, Mrs Chard, this is not at all the sort of matter with which we women are able to deal. I have made it quite plain to Brandon that I am not in the least angry with Bernard for wishing to keep the jewels, and I am most grateful to *you* for telling me of them. I can guess, I think, how difficult you must find it to defy your husband for conscience' sake. I do trust he will not be exceedingly vexed with you!'

Katharine, deeply conscious of Bernard's mocking regard, felt her cheeks grow hot, but said with as much composure as she could: 'That is of no importance at present, ma'am! May I ask what you intend to do now?'

'I was just about to ask Brandon's advice on that head when you came in,' Emma replied ingenuously, and turned again to Bernard. 'Mrs Chard believes, cousin, that she can hoax Bernard into believing that she has the jewels hidden in her portmanteau, and that he will not discover the truth until they are too far away from here to return for them.'

'Very ingenious,' Bernard said with a grin, 'but if I were in his place I'd not leave the house without first making sure that the jewels are safe in my possession, and I'll lay odds he won't either! Better to put them out of his reach once and for all. Give *me* the jewels, Emma, and your lawyer's direction, and I'll carry them to him without delay. Once they are in his charge you can be easy about them.'

'No!' Katharine spoke sharply. 'Miss Crawthorne, he is trying to trick you! He wants the jewels himself!'

Bernard laughed, unmoved by the accusation. 'Doing it a trifle too brown, my dear!' he said jeeringly. 'Just because my brother's a rogue, it don't follow that I'm one, too!'

'I should think not, indeed!' Miss Crawthorne said indignantly. 'Permit me to tell you, ma'am, that I find that remark to be in the worst possible taste.'

'Oh, pay no heed to her, cousin,' Bernard put in lightly. 'She has never liked me above half, have you, Katharine?'

She cast him a speaking glance but made no reply to this. Instead she said earnestly to Miss Crawthorne: 'Ma'am, I implore you, do but consider for a moment! Those jewels are enormously valuable, and dishonest persons would go to any lengths to obtain possession of them. You cannot, you *dare* not, trust any of us!'

'By that token, she would trust nobody at all!'

Bernard said mockingly. 'Perhaps you'd better not give me the jewels, Emma! For all you know, I may intend to ride straight to the coast with them, and fly the country!'

'Pray, Brandon, do not make jest of so serious a charge,' Emma replied earnestly, 'for you must know that nothing anyone could say would make me distrust *you*. As for you, ma'am, I do not know why you gave me the jewels in the first place, or why you are now trying to turn me against Brandon, but let me tell you that whatever your purpose may be, it will not serve! I am going to fetch the jewels immediately, and give them to him so that he may carry them to Mr Spurling.'

She jumped from her chair, and the dog, roused by the note of anger and distress in her voice, bounded to its feet also. She spoke sharply to it, bidding it sit and wait, and reluctantly it obeyed, watching her go from the room and then transferring its suspicious gaze to the two who remained. Bernard leaned back against the table and folded his arms, looking across to Katharine with a knowing grin.

'You might as well have spared your pains, you know,' he informed her conversationally. 'Emma's been wearing the willow for Brandon for years, and as long as she thinks I am he she'll trust me with anything, including the jewels.' He laughed. 'So Brandon means to steal them himself, does he? Well, he took my place last night, so he can't complain if I take his this morning! And there's nothing *you* can do to prevent it. You're in a devilish awkward situation, my girl, and it damned well serves you right!

Katharine paid no heed to this. Turning an

angry, frightened glance upon him, she asked in a low voice: 'How did you contrive to get here?'

'Yes, you didn't bargain for that, did you?' he replied smugly. 'As soon as I stepped out of the chaise last night they overpowered me and trussed me up like a curst chicken. Then Brandon took my hat and overcoat and joined you, while the others carried me off to a damned draughty barn about a mile from here. It took me the best part of the night to get my hands free, and then I had to bide my time, for I couldn't tackle the pair of 'em. Then about an hour ago I heard Elsdale say he was going to meet Brandon, and once he was out of the way I knocked the servant on the head and took one of the horses and came straight here.'

Katharine was staring at him in the blankest astonishment. 'Did you say "Elsdale"?' she asked incredulously.

'Oh, don't play the innocent with me!' he replied impatiently. 'You know dashed well that Elsdale and that confounded groom of his—Wandle—came with Brandon from London. How else could he have got me out of the way? Though I'd give a monkey to know what tale he pitched to Elsdale to persuade him to help, for I'll wager he never told him about the jewels.'

She opened her lips to say that Brandon himself had not known about the jewels, but then changed her mind. It was not important. What was important was the question posed by Lord Elsdale's share in the events of the past twenty-four hours. Had Brandon now gone to fob him off with some lie in order to make his escape with the jewels, or had he, for some inscrutable reason of his own, been merely jesting when he told her he meant to steal them? Of one thing she felt certain. His lordship's honesty could be in no possible doubt.

'I suppose I should have guessed you'd try to tip me the double,' Bernard resumed after a moment, 'but I never thought you'd find a way of doing it. Never occurred to me you'd turn to Brandon, for I fancied the tale he heard from Tillingham had queered the game you were playing in *that* quarter. How did you convince him it wasn't true? Or didn't he care, once he knew about the jewels?'

Katharine looked at him with the utmost distaste. 'How contemptible you are!' she said quietly.

'Mighty high in the instep now, aren't you?' he said with a sneer. 'But let me tell you one thing, my girl! You and Brandon served me a dashed shabby trick last night, and I'm damned if you are going to get the jewels as well. I've been waiting to lay my hands on them ever since Freddy Crawthorne died, and I've no intention of being cheated out of them now.'

Hurried footsteps sounded on the stairs and in the hall, and the door was flung open. Miss Crawthorne burst into the room, saying incoherently: 'I cannot find them! I have looked all over the bedroom, and even in her portmanteau, and they are not there.'

'No, they are not,' Katharine agreed calmly, as Bernard swore and took a pace forward. 'I have hidden them again, and I have not the smallest intention of telling you where.'

'Oh, haven't you?' Bernard said softly, and turned to Emma. 'You see how it is, cousin? As soon as she knew that I had arrived she hid the jewels again in a different place. There never was any intention of giving them up to you.'

'That is absurd!' Katharine said indignantly. 'If it were true I need not have shown them to Miss Crawthorne at all. Oh, believe me, ma'am, I am only trying to help you! Send someone to fetch your lawyer—yes, and the village constable—and in their presence I will gladly tell you where I have hidden the jewels.'

'Oh, this is too much!' Emma tottered across to her chair again and sank into it, and the dog thrust its great muzzle anxiously against her. 'Those jewels belong to me! I insist—no, I *demand*—that you give them to me immediately, or I *will* send for the constable, and have you and your husband placed under arrest, cousin or no!'

'Send for them by all means, ma'am,' Katharine replied, assuming a calmness she did not entirely feel. 'The jewels are perfectly safe where they are, and I have done no wrong in hiding them for their own protection. It *would* be wrong to give them to this man, for that would be aiding him to rob you.'

'How dare you?' Miss Crawthorne's voice shook so much that she found difficulty in enunciating the words. She was trembling with anger, her hands gripping convulsively at the arms of the chair. 'Oh, how dare you make such wicked accusations against him? I have done my best to be civil ever since you and your worthless husband forced yourselves into my house, but now I will tell you to your head, ma'am, that I have never liked or trusted Bernard Chard! He was a spiteful, deceitful little boy, and he became worse as he grew older. He even led my poor brother into all manner of wild dissipation which hastened him into his grave. How two brothers can be so like in looks and so different in character is more than I can understand, but nothing you can say will ever make me trust Bernard, or shake the complete faith I have in Brandon's honesty and kindness. So fetch the jewels immediately and give them to him, or I shall send Joseph at once to summon the constable.'

Katharine had listened with growing dismay to this passionate denunciation, but when Miss Crawthorne paused for breath she turned her head to look at Bernard. He was leaning against the table again, and, far from being discomposed by this accurate and unflattering description of his character, appeared to be deriving considerable amusement from it. Katharine looked from his smirking face to Emma's angry, distressed countenance, and knew that only one course remained open to her. She would have given a great deal to avoid taking it, but Bernard had forced her into a situation from which no other escape was possible. She spoke quickly, before her courage had time to fade.

'Miss Crawthorne,' she said quietly, 'you have judged your two kinsmen very accurately. So accurately, in fact, that I am astonished you have not yet perceived the truth, even though you have seen neither of them for years. *This* man is Bernard Chard. It was Brandon who came here with me last night.'

Bernard straightened abruptly from his lounging position by the table. The self-satisfied smile had faded from his face; his eyes were narrowed and there was a vicious look about his mouth.

'Damn you, Katharine!' he said deliberately. 'I

thought you would do anything rather than admit that.'

'Yes, even to handing you the jewels to make off with,' she retorted scornfully. 'Well, Bernard, I will not! You may search for them if you choose, but I do not think you will find them before Brandon returns.'

'Brandon? Bernard?' Miss Crawthorne's bewilderment was pathetic, overwhelming even her anger. She stared at Katharine, and said in the tone of one groping unwillingly after an unpalatable truth, 'But you are Bernard's wife!'

'No, cousin!' Bernard spoke in a harsh, sneering voice before Katharine could find words with which to answer. 'Neither my wife nor Brandon's! She is merely a wench I took from a London gaming-hell to play the part of my wife, since I knew you would not permit an unmarried man to stay in your house.'

'A gaming-hell? *You* took her——' Emma broke off, looking from one to the other. 'I do not understand!' she added piteously.

'I'll wager you don't, cousin, so let me explain! I told Katharine about the jewels, and promised her a share if she'd help me to find 'em. She seemed willing enough, but I'd forgotten it was Brandon she had a fancy for. He'd been casting out lures to her nearly as long as I had, but there was a rich old nobleman mad for her, too, and Miss Katharine couldn't make up her mind between *his* fortune and her liking for Brandon. I was fool enough to think the jewels had tipped the balance in *my* favour, but she blabbed the whole tale to my brother, and he and two cronies of his waylaid us last night so that he could take my place. They were the "robbers" I told you of.' He paused, studying her stricken face, and then laughed with malicious satisfaction. 'I'm the one you've never trusted, Emma, but your precious Brandon and this little doxy of his have bubbled you finely between them.'

Miss Crawthorne rose slowly to her feet. The dog got up, too, and she grasped its spiked collar as though for support. She was grey-faced with shock, and looked like an old woman.

'Is he speaking the truth?' she asked with difficulty.

Katharine moved her hands in a little, helpless gesture. Half truth and half lies, told in a manner calculated to deal the maximum hurt, Bernard's story seemed impossible to refute. 'It is partly true,' she said wearily, 'and the lies do not matter now. If I denied them you would not believe me. But at least your jewels are safe, for I will not tell you where they are until someone whom you are certain you can trust has been summoned to take charge of them.'

'Now that,' Bernard remarked, 'is where you are mistaken, my dear girl! You are going to tell me where they are, and you are going to tell me now.'

He put his hand into the breast of his coat, and withdrew it holding a pistol. Miss Crawthorne uttered a stifled scream, and the dog lowered its head and growled savagely, its lip lifting to bare powerful fangs.

'I took this pistol from Wandle before I made my escape,' Bernard informed Katharine. 'Thought I might find a excuse to use it on Brandon if we chanced to meet. And if you let that brute make the least move towards me, Emma, I'll put a bullet through its ugly head.'

'No!' Miss Crawthorne's voice was shrill with panic, and she clutched at the dog's collar with both hands. 'In the name of pity, Bernard, not my dog!'

'Keep the brute quiet, then, if you don't want it hurt. I'll not warn you a second time.' He glanced at Katharine. 'I'm waiting, my girl, and I'm getting deuced impatient. Where have you hidden those jewels!'

'I will not tell you!' Her face was paper-white and she was trembling so much that she was obliged to grasp the back of the nearest chair for support, but somehow she found the courage to defy him. 'I do not think you dare use that pistol! You do not know where to find the jewels, and if you were to kill one of us you could not risk staying to search for them.'

'Clever, aren't you?' he sneered, and, taking a quick pace forward, grasped her wrist with his free hand before she could evade him, twisting her arm up cruelly behind her so that she flinched with pain. 'Why, you stubborn little jade, I'll have the truth out of you if I have to break every bone in your body to do it!'

He forced her wrist relentlessly higher, so that a dozen white-hot spears of agony seemed to stab her arm and shoulder and she felt sick and dizzy with pain. She writhed hopelessly in his grip, seeking in vain to ease the unbearable pressure, and uttered a sobbing cry as it was ruthlessly increased. The dog was still growling ferociously, but remained obedient to Emma's restraining hold, her frantic commands to it to be still.

THE RELUCTANT ADVENTURESS 213

The door was flung violently open, and through the tears misting her eyes Katharine saw that it was Brandon who had entered, and cried out again in desperate warning. Then several things happened at once. Bernard let her go as he swung around to discharge the pistol at his brother, and at the same instant Emma released the dog, which launched itself in one mighty leap straight at Bernard. Its crashing impact sent both him and Katharine to the floor, and for a few seconds pandemonium reigned. Bernard yelled to Emma to call off the dog, his panic-stricken voice mingling with the savage snarling of the enraged animal as he struggled frantically to fend off its great jaws. Katharine, trying to get to her feet, cried out again, in sheer terror this time, and then Brandon reached her and lifted her bodily out of harm's way. Half fainting with fright and pain, breathless and shaken from the fall, she clung desperately to him as he bore her across the room and set her gently on her feet by the fireplace.

'Kate!' His voice was low, urgent with concern. 'Kate, are you hurt?'

She shook her head, denying the throbbing agony in her shoulder, and the feeling that she had been bruised and buffeted beyond endurance, aware only of the blessed security of his arms around her. It gave her the courage after a moment or two to turn her head towards the middle of room, and she saw that Miss Crawthorne was again clinging to the dog and trying to quiet it while Lord Elsdale, who had followed Brandon into the room, hauled its victim to his feet and thrust him into a chair. Bernard had succeeded in protecting his face and throat, but his arms had suffered badly in consequence. The sleeves of his coat were torn to rags, and blood was soaking into them and dripping on the floor.

Brandon put Katharine gently into the nearest chair and went forward, saying quietly to Miss Crawthorne: 'I am sorry for this, cousin! I believe I owe my life to that dog of yours for spoiling Bernard's aim, and that is more than I deserve after playing so shabby a trick upon you. Pray believe, though, that I never intended you the least harm.'

Emma, pallid with shock, had dropped into her chair again, one hand still gripping the collar of the now passive dog. She did not look at Brandon, and appeared to have some difficulty in controlling her voice.

'I feel as though I had wandered by chance into Bedlam,' she complained. 'You have treated me abominably, and I wish you would all go away and leave me in peace!'

'We shall do so, very soon now,' he replied soothingly, 'but Bernard cannot go in that state, you know. Perhaps your servant could fetch what is needed, so that his injuries may be tended first.'

'I'll see to it, Captain! You leave it all to me!' The assurance came from a wiry, sharp-faced man who had just come briskly into the room with Joseph hobbling at his heels. He trod across to the chair where Bernard was slumped, white-faced and groaning, and eyed him dispassionately. 'Fair chewed to pieces, ain't he? I've never cared much for dogs myself, specially big brutes like the one yonder, but I feel bound to say as this young fellow got no more than he deserved. Still, I don't bear no grudge for a knock on the head, and he can't be left there bleeding like a stuck pig, that's certain!' He turned to ad-

THE RELUCTANT ADVENTURESS 215

dress Joseph. 'You fetch me a bowl o' water, old 'un, and some clean linen, and mebbe a nip o' brandy if you've got such in the house, and we'll do what we can to fix him up.'

Lord Elsdale, who appeared to be quite accustomed to his servant's oddity of manner, gave up his place beside Bernard and moved towards Katharine. She looked timidly up at him, but was reassured by the friendliness in his eyes.

'I fear you have sustained a severe shock, ma'am,' he said kindly, 'for which I and my servant are largely to blame. Had we not failed lamentably in the part assigned to us you would have been spared a very frightening experience.'

She shook her head, looking at him with a puzzled frown. 'I do not know how you come to be here at all, my lord,' she said unsteadily. 'I supposed you to be still in Wales.'

'We returned to London the day before yesterday. I had informed Brandon that we would be arriving, and that evening he came to see me, a good deal concerned on your behalf. He told me the whole story, and the next morning I went with him to his brother's rooms. When we learned what had happened I naturally offered him any help which lay in my power.' The astonishment in her eyes made him smile, and he added ruefully: "You are thinking, no doubt, that last night's escapade was one in which I should have taken no part? Well, I suppose it would not do to have it generally known, but to tell truth I enjoyed it excessively, and so did Wandle. It reminded us both of adventures we shared with Brandon in Spain.'

'I wish I had known, sir, that you had come with

him,' she said in a low voice. 'I imagined his companions to be persons of a very different sort.'

'Yes, he made us out to be a pair of very desperate characters, I'll be bound!' Elsdale agreed with some amusement. 'It was a great deal too bad of him, but even more deplorable in us to let our prisoner escape. I shall count myself fortunate if Brandon does not call me to account for allowing you to be so misused.'

She smiled perfunctorily at this, but said merely: 'Bernard was angry because I had hidden the jewels again, and because I told Miss Crawthorne who he really was. I do not think I could have held out against him much longer had you not come when you did. I am really not at all brave.'

'I think you are, Kate!' Brandon had returned to her side and now laid his hand briefly on hers. 'In many ways.'

She shook her head, not trusting herself to meet his eyes, and glanced across to Emma, to encounter a look which stabbed her with a faint sense of shock. Anger she was prepared for, even resentment, but not this oddly repellent mixture of naked jealousy and self-righteous disgust.

'Cousin Brandon!' Emma spoke sharply, in a cold voice so different from her usual diffidence that he turned to her in astonishment. 'I will endure no more of this! Be good enough to leave my house, and take your—take that young woman with you.'

For a moment he continued to stare at her, surprise giving way to anger, and then he said in a voice as cold as her own: 'I think you forget, Emma, that were it not for Katharine you would have been robbed of a fortune.'

THE RELUCTANT ADVENTURESS   217

'I am sensible of that, and I shall be quite willing to pay her adequately in recognition of it!' Emma's tone was in itself an insult. 'But I will not have her in my house.'

Katharine laid her hand quickly on Brandon's arm, checking his furious retort. She looked steadily across at Miss Crawthorne, her face very pale.

'I seek no reward, ma'am,' she said in a level voice. 'I will fetch the jewels to you before I go.'

She got up from the chair, and, though she had never felt so humiliated in her life, pride kept her head high and her step firm as she went out of the room. With the same desperate calm she climbed the stairs and went along the corridor and across the dressing-room to the bedchamber, but when she reached the window the stiff old casement resisted all her efforts to shift it. The pain in her maltreated shoulder had subsided now to a dull ache, but every movement of the arm hurt her and she could not open the window with only one hand. The small defeat broke her hard-won composure, and with a sob she leaned her forehead against the stone mullion of the window while tears filled her eyes.

The sound of a familiar footstep jerked her upright again, and as Brandon came into the room she turned quickly away to hide her tears, saying with a catch in her voice: 'The jewels are out there! I hid the box in the ivy below the window, but now the casement is too stiff for me.'

While he forced open the stubborn window and leaned out to retrieve the casket she went to fetch her outdoor garments from the cupboard. Dropping the bonnet on the bed, she began to struggle into the pelisse, biting her lip as pain once more stabbed fiercely through arm and shoulder. Brandon dropped the jewel-box carelessly on to the nearest chair and came quickly to help her. Then he turned her very gently to face him.

'Kate,' he said quietly, 'you have every right to be angry with me. I am exceedingly angry with myself.'

'Angry?' Surprise tricked her into looking up at him. 'But why?'

'Because I doubted you! Because even last night, when you had told me of the desperation which prompted you to agree to Bernard's plan, I still could not entirely rid myself of the suspicion that those jewels were a temptation you would be unable to resist. So I pretended that I meant to steal them, and then left them with you, hoping with all my heart that you would take the opportunity of giving them to Emma, and so prove your honesty beyond all possibility of doubt. But I should not have needed proof, Kate! I should have trusted you without it.'

'No, why should you? Knowing the kind of man my uncle is, hearing the lying tales which were told about me, and which I had unknowingly admitted to be true——'

'Tales which originated with my brother,' he interrupted her. 'That alone should have warned me to place no dependence upon them. I offered you my friendship, assured you that you might depend upon it, and yet failed you at the first test. And again today! It was my fault that Bernard was able to hurt and frighten you so—yes, and that you were so bitterly insulted by Emma! Kate, can you ever forgive me?'

'Yes, gladly, if there were anything to forgive, but there is not.' She paused, looking up into his face, but after a moment gave a little sigh and turned away. 'This is all to no purpose. We had better go!'

'No, wait!' He caught her hand to stop her. 'We are not going until one more question has been answered. Kate, will you marry me?'

'Why?' she asked with a hint of bitterness. 'Because you feel that you owe it to me? Because the only alternative is a return to my uncle's house? Oh, Brandon, let me go! Can you not see that the one thing I cannot endure is your pity?'

'Not pity,' he said quietly. 'God knows it was never that, even when I first asked you to be my wife. I tried then to be honest with you, because I believed that the life you wanted was one which I could not endure, even for your sake. I know now that I was mistaken. That you are more important to me than anything else in the world.' He watched a dawning joy and wonder drive the unhappiness from her face, and laughed gently, and took her in his arms. 'My sweet, foolish Kate, do you not know I love you? That I would never have said such cruel, wounding things to you that day had I not been half out of my mind with jealousy?'

A few minutes later Lord Elsdale and Miss Crawthorne, engaged in awkward, desultory conversation in the bare, dusty hall, were interrupted by the sound of footsteps on the stairs, and, turning in that direction, saw Brandon coming down towards them. In one hand he carried a sturdy, brass-bound box. The other arm was laid protectively around Katharine's shoulders, and one glance at the quiet radiance in the girl's face told the watchers all they needed to know. She looked an entirely different person from the pale, defiant woman who had left them so short a while ago. They reached the foot of the stairs, and Brandon held the box out to his cousin.

'Here are the jewels, Emma,' he said quietly. 'I do not think it likely that we shall ever meet again.'

She took the box without looking in it. There was a bright spot of colour burning in either cheek, and her mouth was set in a hard, implacable line. For an instant her glance met Katharine's, and the girl knew, with a swift surge of compassion, that though Emma held a fortune in her hands, she was herself by far the richer of the two. Then without a word Emma turned her back upon them, and with the dog padding at her heels went quickly across the hall to a door on the farther side, and passed through and slammed it behind her.

'I have sent Wandle for a carriage to convey Bernard to the inn,' Elsdale remarked into the uncomfortable silence, 'and to arrange for a doctor to see him there.' He glanced from Brandon to Katharine, and a smile glimmered in his eyes. 'I think perhaps I had better take charge of matters here. The chaise is waiting, and no doubt you are anxious to be on your way.'

'You're the best of good fellows, Robert,' Brandon said with a laugh, 'and now I am going to impose even further on your good nature. We are going to Mallows, and I shall be most deeply in your debt if, as soon as you return to London, you will obtain a special licence and send it to me there.'

'Nothing could give me greater pleasure! This is

excellent news indeed, though I will not pretend to any great degree of surprise.' He held out his hand to Katharine and she put hers into it, looking up shyly to meet his smile. 'Judith, I know, will be delighted! She had been hoping for this from the moment you met. As for the licence, we shall bring it to you ourselves. It is not to be thought of that our two closest friends should be married, and we not there to wish them happiness.'

He raised Katharine's hand to his lips, clapped Brandon on the shoulder, and accompanied them out to the waiting chaise. A minute or two later, as the carriage made its way along the neglected drive, Katharine said in a low voice:

'Lord Elsdale is exceedingly kind! I had quite made up my mind to it that after all that has happened I should never see Judith again, but he spoke just now as though there was no reason why we should not continue friends.'

'It will not yet be possible for her to receive you in London, my love,' Brandon warned her gently, taking her hand in his, 'for too many people know that you were at the curst gaming-house. The world must be given time to forget that, and to find fresh affairs to gossip over, before we can return to town.' He broke off as his fingers encountered the wedding-ring she still wore, and with a quick frown he drew it off and, letting down the window, tossed it out. It gleamed for an instant in the sun, and then was lost in the tangled undergrowth bordering the drive. He closed the window again and turned to take Katharine in his arms, looking down into her face.

'I'll make you no rash promises, Kate,' he said

ruefully. 'I shall probably be a damnable husband, and set the whole county by the ears time and again. Will you be able to bear with me, do you think?'

For a moment or two she was silent, as though pondering the question, a little smile playing about her lips, her eyes downcast so that the long lashes hid their expression from him.

'That is if we live in Worcestershire, is it not?' she asked at length, a hint of mischief in her voice. 'But you told me once there was an alternative to that.'

'Kate, do you mean it?' His arms tightened about her; there was a sudden note of exultation in his voice. 'God knows I am willing to try to become what you desire me to be, but to take you adventuring with me, to know that you come gladly—ah, that would be happiness indeed!'

'To be with you always, Brandon. That is the sum of my desire,' she said softly, and lifted her face for his kiss. A new wisdom told her that it would be idle to try to change him, to seek to curb his adventurous spirit within the conventional bounds she had been taught to admire. She would go with him, gladly, as he had said, until the day came when, of his own free will, he chose to return to the home which had awaited him for so long.

Sylvia Thorpe

Sparkling novels of love and conquest set against the colorful background of historic England. Here are stories you will savor word by word, page by spellbinding page into the wee hours of the night.

☐ BEGGAR ON HORSEBACK	23091-0	1.50
☐ CAPTAIN GALLANT	Q2709	1.50
☐ FAIR SHINE THE DAY	23229-8	1.75
☐ THE GOLDEN PANTHER	23006-6	1.50
☐ THE RELUCTANT ADVENTURESS	P2578	1.25
☐ ROGUE'S COVENANT	23041-4	1.50
☐ ROMANTIC LADY	Q2910	1.50
☐ THE SCANDALOUS LADY ROBIN	Q2934	1.50
☐ THE SCAPEGRACE	P2663	1.25
☐ THE SCARLET DOMINO	23220-4	1.50
☐ THE SILVER NIGHTINGALE	P2626	1.25
☐ THE SWORD AND THE SHADOW	22945-9	1.50
☐ SWORD OF VENGEANCE	23136-4	1.50
☐ TARRINGTON CHASE	Q2843	1.50

Buy them at your local bookstores or use this handy coupon for ordering:

FAWCETT PUBLICATIONS, P.O. Box 1014, Greenwich Conn. 06830

Please send me the books I have checked above. Orders for less than 5 books must include 60c for the first book and 25c for each additional book to cover mailing and handling. Orders of 5 or more books postage is Free. I enclose $_____ in check or money order.

Name_____

Address_____

City_____ State/Zip_____

Please allow 4 to 5 weeks for delivery. This offer expires 6/78.

A-24

HELEN MacINNES

Helen Macinnes's bestselling suspense novels continue to delight her readers and many have been made into major motion pictures. Here is your chance to enjoy all of her exciting novels, by simply filling out the coupon below.

☐ ABOVE SUSPICION	23101-1	1.75
☐ AGENT IN PLACE	23127-5	1.95
☐ ASSIGNMENT IN BRITTANY	22958-0	1.95
☐ DECISION AT DELPHI	C2790	1.95
☐ THE DOUBLE IMAGE	22787-1	1.75
☐ FRIENDS AND LOVERS	X2714	1.75
☐ HORIZON	23123-2	1.50
☐ I AND MY TRUE LOVE	Q2559	1.50
☐ MESSAGE FROM MALAGA	X2820	1.75
☐ NEITHER FIVE NOR THREE	X2912	1.75
☐ NORTH FROM ROME	Q2441	1.50
☐ PRAY FOR A BRAVE HEART	X2907	1.75
☐ REST AND BE THANKFUL	X2860	1.75
☐ THE SALZBURG CONNECTION	X2686	1.75
☐ THE SNARE OF THE HUNTER	X2808	1.75
☐ THE VENETIAN AFFAIR	X2743	1.75
☐ WHILE STILL WE LIVE	23099-6	1.95

Buy them at your local bookstores or use this handy coupon for ordering:

FAWCETT PUBLICATIONS, P.O. Box 1014, Greenwich Conn. 06830

Please send me the books I have checked above. Orders for less than 5 books must include 60c for the first book and 25c for each additional book to cover mailing and handling. Orders of 5 or more books postage is Free. I enclose $_____ in check or money order.

Mr/Mrs/Miss_____

Address_____

City_____ State/Zip_____

Please allow 4 to 5 weeks for delivery. This offer expires 6/78.

A-8